My Prisoner

MY
PRISONER

by
Janey Jimenez
as told to
Ted Berkman

SHEED ANDREWS AND McMEEL, INC.
Subsidiary of Universal Press Syndicate
Kansas City

Library of Congress Cataloging in Publication Data

Jimenez, Janey.
    My prisoner.

    1. Jimenez, Janey. 2. Correctional personnel—
United States—Biography. 3. Hearst, Patricia,
1954-   4. Crime and criminals—California—Biog-
raphy. 5. Trials (Robbery)—California.
I. Berkman, Ted, joint author. II. Title.
HV9468.J55A35   365'.43'0924 [B]   77-21859
ISBN 0-8362-0739-4

1

The door from the cellblock area swung open and, half-hidden by a bulky matron, the wispy figure of a girl appeared. Her short-cut hair was a shapeless tangle. Battered blue corduroys, too baggy for her narrow hips, flopped aimlessly around her ankles. She wore no bra; under her bright red sweater were the outlines of small, almost childish breasts.

I turned to my chief. "That can't be Patty Hearst!"

"Yes, it is."

"But she's so tiny!" I stared again. This was all wrong. The FBI "Wanted" photo, taken from Patty's high school graduation picture, had shown a smiling attractive girl with soft wavy hair framing a wide-mouthed cheerful face. From the strong, regular features I had expected a fairly tall person, at least matching my own five feet three. And from the excited chatter earlier that morning at the Marshals Service, I had built up the mental image of a hard-swearing, gum-chewing lady bandit out of *Bonnie and Clyde*. This girl, with her thin, taut face and puny shoulders, looked about as threatening as a baby rabbit.

We were in the women's section of the San Mateo County Jail in Redwood City: John Brophy, chief deputy

U.S. marshal for Northern California, and I, the newest member of his staff. It was September 29, 1975. Patty Hearst, picked up by the FBI eleven days earlier in nearby San Francisco, had been ordered to undergo a gynecological examination at Stanford Hospital. The escorting officer would be me, Janey Jimenez, sworn in just two hours before as the first deputy marshal of either my sex or minority background to serve in the area; fresh out of college a year earlier; at twenty-two, one of the country's youngest deputies and certainly its most nervous.

I had worked briefly as a corrections officer, but had no real experience in law enforcement. Transporting a prisoner in public was a dangerous procedure requiring armed support; I had never carried a gun, much less fired one. Even getting a prisoner into handcuffs was a notoriously tricky moment; there were techniques for overcoming resistance, but nobody had as yet told me about them. Against Patty's status of "most wanted," I shaped up as "least qualified."

I couldn't keep staring forever. Sheriffs and guards were milling around; a middle-aged woman was being fingerprinted at the booking desk. It was time to get down to business. What trouble could I possibly have with this small, silent waif?

Still, the talk of her exploits lingered. She had handled an automatic rifle, the deputies said, like a veteran. What if she pulled some sudden judo trick? My eight hours of training in a Matrons' Course shrank in my mind to eight minutes. The rabbity look could be a lure, a pose to throw me off guard. I was about to step into a cage with a lioness, and I felt about as equipped for the task as a poodle-trainer.

But I couldn't let the prisoner know that. Or my chief, either. Brophy, a crisp-mannered little Irishman, was watching intently: from all accounts a decent, generous man who'd been through the mill himself as a boxer and marine, but a stickler for professional standards.

I took a few steps forward and confronted Patty. "You know," I told her in what I hoped was a firm voice, "I'm going to have to search you."

She nodded without apparent interest.

I wasn't quite sure whether Patty was to get routine treatment, or special handling. Either way, I could see myself in trouble. If I gave her a thorough "shake-down"—everything short of a strip-search—Brophy might call it off as unnecessary with this prisoner, and leave me red-faced. But if I didn't, I might look even worse.

I told her to stand with her legs well apart, and spread out her arms: standard opening for what we call a "frisk search." After emptying her pockets, I went carefully over her body: around the neck; then, from the back, up and down the arms; over the ribs, breast, waistline; finally down the buttocks and legs, into the crotch. From the unmanicured state of her nails, I suspected that her personal grooming had fallen into neglect. Streaks of auburn discolored her chestnut-brown hair.

Patty didn't say anything, although she looked a little startled when I proceeded methodically to go through her hair. That's where prisoners often hide drugs as well as blades, wires, pencils, bobby pins . . . a host of small objects useful for picking handcuff-locks. When I got to her ears, Patty spoke up: "I've never had to go through all this before." Her voice was flat, detached, with a kind of hollow echo-chamber quality, as if coming from

7

another world.

"I'm sorry," I answered, "but you know, this is what I'm supposed to do." I didn't want to leave any question in her mind about my being able to do it.

I picked up the pack of cigarettes she had been carrying and ripped them open, probing inside.

"Oh, come on," she said. "What are you doing?" As if to ask: What can possibly be in there?

"You'd be surprised what people hide in cigarettes."

Patty nodded thoughtfully. There was nothing sullen or hostile about her; just a calm, remote curiosity. The "tough bitch" that one of the deputies had forecast had not materialized; at no point did she engage in the mocking taunts of hard-core girl prisoners, who will punctuate a legitimate shakedown with jeers of "You really love touching me, don't you. . . . Now I see why you dig this job. . . . So this is how you get your kicks!"

She remained cool—cooler than I was—through the exam. Nor did she flinch from the handcuffs. I was so intent on getting them on right—snug enough to prevent wriggling free, but not so tight as to impede circulation—that I did not at that time notice how tiny her wrists were.

We went down by special elevator to the basement, where a cluster of deputies including Chief Brophy piled into a car along with Patty and me. Federal law requires at least two officers to accompany a prisoner in transit. Patty had a lot more than that. Cars with armed deputies rode immediately ahead of and behind us, and there were more security vehicles waiting at the hospital.

During the ten-mile trip, Patty continued to surprise me. We passed a cluster of buildings in a courtyard, screened off from the road by dense foliage, and Patty remarked that she had gone to school there; it was a "really beautiful place." She did no ranting about the Establishment. When I sprang forward to offer a light for her cigarette—not so much out of politeness as to keep control of any lighted matches in the car—she responded with a soft, civil "Thank you." For an alleged revolutionary and despite her hand-me-down appearance, she was displaying a disconcerting degree of old-fashioned delicacy.

Then, at some moment I cannot pinpoint, she seemed suddenly to slip away. I looked over at her, and although of course she was still bodily present, I could swear Patty Hearst was no longer there. Beside me was a silent mummylike figure, staring straight ahead, seemingly unaware of my scrutiny or even of my presence. I remember thinking to myself: Is this the awesome, famous Patty Hearst? She seems more like a zombie, a ghost; I'm not sure anyone is here with me at all.

For a moment my own presence, too, seemed unreal. When I first entered the prison system in October of 1974, Patty Hearst was the last thing on my mind. I had come up from a rugged *chicano* background, one of six children in a working-class American family of Mexican descent living in the Los Angeles suburb of Van Nuys. Patty's grandfather was the legendary Lord of San Simeon, millionaire founder of a newspaper empire; my grandmother, in flight from marauding guerrilla bands, had trudged and hitchhiked nearly one thousand miles across the face of Mexico to sanctuary on the U.S. side of the border.

At eight I was baby-sitting and mowing lawns; by

thirteen I had lost my father. All through high school I cooked and washed around the house, and took whatever outside jobs I could get. Patty Hearst and I are only a year apart in age (I'm older). But when she was frolicking along the Hong Kong waterfront in the spring of 1971, I was sweating through a sixty-hour week at San Diego State College, carrying a full load of credits and a student-aide job with a government defense subcontractor.

My original goal was to work as an interpreter in the prison system, aiding fellow *chicanos* who, for want of educational and economic opportunity, were often caught up in the toils of the law before they knew what was happening to them. So I majored in the Spanish language and Mexican history, and soon after graduation landed a job at the Metropolitan Correction Center in San Diego, a new federal institution specializing in short-term offenders. For several months I acted as receptionist-interpreter while attending courses in correctional techniques.

Then I heard there were openings coming up in the Marshals Service, the federal enforcement arm for U.S. courts and agencies, charged mainly with transporting prisoners and providing security for witnesses and judges. There were some eighteen hundred deputy marshals around the country, of whom only a handful were women. As a deputy, I could be closer to the seats of authority, perhaps move up to a position where I could exercise some influence on behalf of my people. And the improved salary would be helpful in financing studies toward a graduate degree.

I took the tests in March, received an appointment in May, and after turning down an opening in Boston was offered a post in the fall where my long training in Spanish would be useful: San Francisco. I would be the only bilingual female deputy in California; the two women members of the Service in San Diego were *anglos*.

On September 18, as I was handing in my notice at MCC, I heard that Patty Hearst had just been arrested in the Bay area. I shrugged off the news as being of no concern to me. By the time I reported to the Marshals Service, she would probably be well into arraignment and trial procedures; and I wàs scheduled to begin my new job with an intensive training program in Georgia.

I arrived in San Francisco on the morning of September 29, was sworn in at 9:45 A.M., and found myself suddenly pitched into a *macho* cloak-and-dagger world of guns, electronic surveillance gadgets, and security codes. There were no other women in the deputies' room. I felt like the greenhorn of all time—and undoubtedly looked it. Conscious of curious masculine stares, I took refuge in the duties manual on my desk.

At 10:30 I was summoned to Chief Deputy Brophy's office. Brophy was on the phone, saying something about a double check on the transmitters. On the wall behind him, an assistant was marking up a diagram of the approaches to Stanford Hospital, with car routes and guard posts laid out. A subdued excitement was in the air.

Brophy turned to me. "You'll have to take somebody to the hospital. Ever done that before?"

"A couple of times. At MCC."

"Okay. Get your gear."

Back at my desk in the Criminal Section, I learned that the "somebody" was Patty Hearst. The most prominent prisoner in the country—on my very first day! I felt a flush of panic.

I was hardly what you would call an expert on the Hearst case. Like millions of other Americans, I was vaguely aware of its highlights: A very rich girl, daughter of a publishing tycoon, had been snatched from the campus apartment she shared with her fiancé in Berkeley by one of the underground radical groups that flourished in the Bay area. There was some claim that she was being held as a "prisoner of war," but the name of her captors—the "Symbionese Liberation Army"—hadn't rung any bells with me. An oddity or two about the make-up of the band remained in my mind: a black "General Field Marshal" named Cinque, an unusual number of women, all white.

I knew there had been a series of taped communiqués demanding food-distribution money from Patty's father, Randolph Hearst, topped by the incredible announcement from Patty that she had joined her revolutionary abductors. And then the bombshell: every paper in America had pictures of Patty as "Tania," brandishing a carbine during a holdup at a district branch of the Hibernia Bank in San Francisco. Soon afterward there was a hideous gun battle in Los Angeles—featured over live television—in which five hundred police wiped out four women and two men of the SLA. From then on, Patty became the FBI's star fugitive until they caught up with her and the two surviving members of the original band in San Francisco. I remembered an ethnic twist: with Patty when the FBI burst into her apartment was a Japanese-American roommate, Wendy Yoshimura.

By that time, I had an impression of Patty that was

probably pretty general around the country—a blur of automatic rifles and tough-talking tapes, willfulness and angry rebellion—but very little factual knowledge.

What I did know about, weirdly enough, was the Hearst Castle at San Simeon. In fact, I was something of a nut on the subject. Our high school class used to visit it every year, and I'd been there three times. It was the most fantastic place I'd ever seen, a marshmallow sundae of a palace with Roman baths, baronial halls and gorgeous chapels brought piece by piece from Europe to be reassembled here. I once did a long report on the main building, full of historical details dredged up from libraries. And even after finishing high school I went back for several days, compelled to poke into corners I hadn't seen before, driven by a search for I don't know what.

At first I hadn't connected the storybook castle with the fugitive girl wanted for bank robbery; in fact, I was surprised to learn that the fabulous Mr. Hearst had any surviving family. Now here I was, side by side with the living princess of the castle. How would we two, similar in age but planets apart in practically every other respect, get along?

One thing seemed clear: I should avoid getting personally involved. Not only government rules but instinct warned against it. I had worked hard and crashed some rough barriers to arrive at this first assignment. Young, female, and from an often-disparaged minority group, I had yet to prove myself. Many eyes were upon me, many hands would not be reluctant to give me a downward push.

2

The hospital visit had been ordered by the jail doctor for diagnosis of excessive vaginal bleeding. Patty was eating poorly and suffering headaches. Her weight had dropped from its prekidnap norm of 110 to less than 100, and the medical people were worried.

We checked in, were assigned to an examining room, and then ran into a snag. The hospital required a release before starting tests; Patty wasn't signing anything except in the presence of a legal adviser. Those were her instructions, she insisted; and nobody could budge her. In vain I tried to explain that the tests were in her own interest; the government couldn't be responsible if she fainted away in her cell.

She just shook her head: no lawyer, no signature. Calls were put in to the Hearst Corporation, but the people she wanted couldn't be reached. So we settled down, alone in that cold bare windowless examining room, to wait.

I said "alone," but that was only in theory—especially for the first couple of hours. It seemed that everybody in Stanford Hospital wanted to get a look at Patty. From their attitude, she could have been an animal on display. Our cubicle was one of a series running down a long corridor that was set off by heavy double doors. Faces kept appearing at the glass panels of the doors, straining for a glimpse of the notorious new patient. Bolder personnel invented "errands" that would take them into the corridor. But with deputies ringing our door, and no windows to peek through, it didn't do the celebrity-hunters any good. The deputies brought us coffee, and more coffee. Patty sat there, chain-smoking and gulping it down.

Inevitably—we'd gone through two pots of coffee—we both needed the rest room. We notified the deputies outside and started down the hall. By the time we'd gone ten feet, there was a crowd tailing us. People popped out of sickrooms, nursing stations, closets: everywhere we looked, there were staring faces.

It was scary. Various fringe groups had been vowing vengeance against Patty. I saw her go pale, and I couldn't blame her. Anybody could have slipped into that hospital as a visitor, changed in a washroom into attendants' whites, and be stalking her down the hall—with a gun in his pocket or a knife up his sleeve. It wouldn't have to be a man, either. Were all those uniformed ladies scurrying through the corridors actually nurses? Was anybody checking their I.D.'s?

I knew something Patty didn't, from the deputy who had been our driver. Several threats and suspicious calls had come in to the hospital, asking for details of the floor layout. One was attributed to the Black Panthers.

Patty hesitated. I took her firmly by the arm and started steering her back. There was no point in setting up an open target.

This terror of the unknown, the suspicion that every shadowy corner could conceal a gunman, that a name carelessly dropped in court might lead to murderous reprisal, was to hang over Patty's subsequent trial, forcing her ultimately to take damaging refuge in the Fifth Amendment.

Back in the examining room, Nature resumed her demands. We didn't have much choice. I asked one of the deputies outside to have a bedpan sent in.

Well . . . I've been through some pretty peculiar experiences in my life, but taking turns with a stranger on a bedpan! I was beginning to feel like a prisoner myself.

It was a funny way to start a relationship, but in a sense that icy bedpan drew us together. After the mutual exposure to that dignity-robbing moment, we could hardly go back to the distance of the guardian-prisoner connection.

We had a little difficulty finding neutral ground for conversation; under the circumstances, Patty's troubles were out of bounds. Then Patty asked where I came from and found out I was a newcomer to San Francisco. From then on the questions flowed: What did I think of her hometown? Had I found a place to live yet? Did I notice how differently people dressed up here?

Soon we were comparing notes on San Diego State versus the campus at Berkeley, and the courses we had majored in. Patty was big on foreign cultures and art history; she had done a lot of traveling, including puttering around among archaeological digs in Greece.

But—her momentary animation dropped away—she wasn't doing much traveling now. At the jail in Redwood City, she was catching up on her reading. And crocheting. She was finding that very easy on the nerves, a good way to chew up time.

Somehow, no doubt along with one of our many vis-

16

itors, a moth had gotten into the room. It was flitting all over the place: settling on Patty's shoulder, then swooping down to investigate my shoe. We decided to capture the moth: at first, with ladylike reserve, fluttering our hands through the air; then, with all-out abandon.

Seconds later we were whirling around the room like a pair of dervishes, hands outstretched after the elusive moth, in dead earnest and at the same time giggling our heads off. The moth was driving us nuts; it was our quarry, tormentor—and playmate. At that moment I recognized in Patty Hearst a kindred spirit. We shared the same penchant for off-the-wall foolery, the same perception of humor in the absurd.

Then the door opened: our moth darted out, and the man Patty had been waiting for, at long last, came in. He was John Knudsen, from the Hearst Corporation; and he was as quick in reviewing the release Patty had to sign as he had been slow in arriving. Within minutes she was ready for the doctor.

The gynecologist came in: a slim, nervous man in his forties. Apparently it had been decided that no nurse would be allowed to accompany him; I would have to fill that role. He told me where to place the bedding and to get Patty undressed.

Helping Patty out of her clothes and into her white surgical gown, I couldn't help noticing again how extremely thin she was. The bones stuck out of her skin. Also, my hunch about a lapse in her grooming was confirmed. Her legs and armpits were unshaven.

As she lay down on the table, I saw a slight trembling. The doctor came in, adjusted her feet to the stirrups; and now her legs were really shaking. She was fighting for self-control.

"I'm not going to hurt you," the doctor assured her, pressing gently to push her legs apart. Patty gave no sign of believing him.

Hadn't she ever had this kind of examination before? Yes, yes. Patty nodded.

So he went ahead, probing with his gloved hand into her vagina. Patty cringed, wriggled away. She shook her head desperately, closed her eyes, bit into her lower lip.

And that's when it happened. Suddenly she let out a piercing wail, and the tears gushed forth. I have never seen a dam burst, but that was the image that crossed my mind.

The doctor tried to hold her still. "Please, Miss Hearst, relax. I can't examine you if you fight me. It will just take a moment."

"Oh, my God," Patty sobbed. "Oh, my God." She struggled for an instant more, then went slack. I had never seen anyone so beaten, crumpled, totally helpless. She lay without moving on the examining table, eyes vacant, curled up like a foetus.

The doctor told her he was finished, she could sit up. And the tears started pouring forth again, uncontrollably.

I had seen women disintegrate on the examining table before, although never to such an extreme. Mostly it had been Mexican girls at MCC, picked up as illegal aliens and then subjected to what is at best a humiliating probe. For them the tension was compounded by the Mexican obsession, passed down from generation to generation, with virginity.

But Patty was not Mexican. Nor was she likely to be a sexual innocent, in view of her general social sophistication and her long engagement to Steven Weed.

Somehow, for me the feeling of "rape victim" filled the room. Instinctively I felt she was responding to some earlier, forcible violation of her body, the memory of which had been thrust upon her—and that it was a memory she could not endure. At that time, no public mention had been made of Patty's treatment at the hands of her abductors—it was not until several months later that her claim of having been assaulted by SLA "soldier" Willie Wolfe and his "Field Marshal," Cinque, went into the trial record. Patty's blacking-out response, when faced with recollections too cruel to bear, would become familiar to me in the months ahead. Never adequately illuminated by her counsel, it would be a major factor in alienating the Hearst jury.

As the doctor left the room, I went to her and cradled her head in my arms. For an instant it occurred to me that I was stepping out of my guardian role, not acting strictly according to the book; even correction officers, much less marshals, are urged to avoid "overly emotional involvement" with offenders. And I wasn't sure how she would react, whether she would still be so wounded as to repulse any human contact. But she was a human being, a woman, and a contemporary, in distress. I had to let her know she was not alone.

Patty clung to me like a child. She cried and cried.

I handed her a Kleenex and helped her wipe her nose. "C'mon," I said. "Time to get dressed. I'll get you some coffee, and you'll be all right."

Then I took my prisoner back to her jail.

In the months to come, I would be officially charged with Patty's custody, responsible for seeing that she remained our prisoner—and that no harm came to her. I

19

would be at her side as shadow and companion, keeper and protector, during long drives to and from courthouse and jail, through endless hours of trial testimony and the welcome breaks of recesses, joining in her moments of laughter on the highways and her days of anguish under treatment in Sequoia Hospital. Every morning I locked her into handcuffs, and even after leaving the Marshals Service in the summer of 1976, I stayed in constant touch with Patty by telephone and visits.

My log books show we were in close contact for some 350 hours—or about as much time as a therapist would have spent with Patty putting in three sessions a week for a whole year. The intensity of our association was unique. Patty and I were squeezed together, pressure-cooker style, because both of us were cut off from practically everyone else, isolated in a special universe of our own where we were dependent on each other for company and diversion—or, as we frequently if inelegantly put it, "to keep from going nuts."

What I got was a woman-to-woman close-up view, uninhibited by medical or legal formalities. Either alone with Patty or with silent bodyguards in the background, I have seen her in every conceivable mood: a Patty not on guard in any sense, away from the lunatic threats of the SLA, the prodding of the FBI, the badgering of the press and the coaching of her attorneys. Without ever seeking it, I've had a backstage seat at the Patty Hearst drama: partner in the intimacies of girl talk, witness to her unrehearsed revelations about her parents, prosecutors, sexual attitudes, and SLA abductors.

The Patty Hearst I came to know is a far cry from either the devil-caricature perpetrated by the SLA or the demure angel fashioned by her lawyers. She laughs easily, weeps when she is hurt, is quick to sympathy and almost fanatic about fairness. She can also be cutting, fussy, pampered and absurdly suggestible.

This very human Patty was one the jury never saw. Yet her character and credibility, her motives and mental state, became the heart of the legal case. Everybody agreed on what she had done, physically—the photos establishing her presence during the Hibernia Bank raid were undisputed—but nobody could say why she had done it. Most of the panel felt they had not been allowed to see more than the tip of the iceberg; their exasperation was reflected in their verdict. I know because after the trial they told me so. As the only woman deputy on a case with a predominantly female jury, I was frequently assigned to evening guard duty with the panel; later I was entrusted with many confidences.

The jurors, unable to figure out the central personality in the case, were left with a host of unanswered questions. Was Patty ruthless revolutionary, or abused victim? Did she willingly join the SLA, or march with them only at gunpoint? Which psychiatrists were to be believed: those who likened Patty to a battered war prisoner, or those who saw her as a symbol of antiparental revolt, delighting in reckless adventure?

What to make of Patty's sex life? Was she a supersophisticate bouncing casually from lover to lover—or a serious young woman who had committed herself to a long-term relationship and was engaged to be married? Promiscuous, or decidedly discriminating? Was Willie Wolfe of the SLA actually her tutor-sweetheart—or an irresponsible sloganeering rapist? Did Patty share the taste of some females among her captors for black sexual partners like "Cinque," who adopted the name of a mutinous nineteenth-century slave?

Baffled, the jurors fell back on the tangibles of photos, tape recordings, documents—and voted to convict. They have been plagued by their decision ever since. Today most of them have swung around to Patty's side; nearly all are haunted by the nagging intuition that if Patty had been presented to them more clearly, as a recognizable person rather than an enigma, they would have acquitted her.

Just how this came about—the seemingly inescapable combination of forces that closed in to separate Patty from those who had to judge her—would take shape for me as the hidden "detective story" of the Hearst case, to be pieced together from fragments of observation buttressed by masses of trial testimony. I would also find many clues outside the courtroom, in our current national values, our tastes in entertainment, and above all in the conflict between parents and children that has rocked America since the middle 1960s.

For Patty, of course, the story is far from over. Although she no longer faces additional charges in Los Angeles, her release on bail in the north is strictly temporary, with a seven-year prison term ahead unless an Appeals Court rules otherwise. And no matter what the court does, she is in a sense not likely ever to be free; to some degree she will be a prisoner for the rest of her life, plagued by private scars and public notoriety.

Meanwhile, I feel obliged to set down my account, if only in the interest of the tormented jurors and the hundreds of people who wrote to me about the case; never, I suspect, has such a wide range of individuals been drawn into such passionate entanglement with the destiny of a total stranger. My portrait of Patty may challenge your previous impressions. But in all fairness perhaps you should give it a chance—because you won't find it anywhere else.

3

After our trip to Stanford Hospital in late September of 1975, Patty Hearst's future was not even a matter of distant speculation on my horizon. I had no reason to assume I would ever see Patty again, or that the adventure at the hospital would be anything but an isolated episode. And I had more immediate personal concerns: within a few days I was flying across the country to Glynco, Georgia, to begin the thirteen-week training program that would prepare me for the responsibilities of a deputy U.S. marshal.

The Federal Law Enforcement Training Center brought together novice marshals with recruits from such agencies as the Secret Service and the FBI to study search-warrant procedures, self-defense techniques, photography, interviewing witnesses, and other aspects of criminalistics. Then the new deputies would go on to Marshals School for specialized instruction in first aid, riot control, and the supervision of sequestered juries. Weaponry was an important part of the course; we would have to become proficient in handling shotguns—there was a skeet layout—as well as the .38 revolver.

With ten lady trainees scattered among more than

three hundred men, the females at the center were as conspicuous as we would have been at West Point or a marine boot camp. Instructors weren't giving anything away to those beginners who wore, or sometimes wore, skirts. I had to knock myself out just to keep pace with the class. Very soon I lost track of the Hearst case and everything else that wasn't built into our daily routine.

I returned to San Francisco in late December, but it wasn't until a couple of weeks after New Year's of 1976 that I was assigned to pick up Patty again. By this time she had been a prisoner in San Mateo County Jail in Redwood City for four months, and the government had sorted out its accusations against her. She faced prosecution by the state in Los Angeles on a complex of charges growing out of a shooting incident on May 16, 1975, at Mel's Sporting Goods Store there, where she had provided covering fire for the SLA's husband-and-wife team, Bill and Emily Harris. But first she would go before a federal judge and jury in San Francisco for her part a month earlier in the Hibernia Bank holdup, indicted on double counts of armed bank robbery and the use of a firearm in the commission of a felony. Her trial date had been fixed for February 4, and I was assigned to be her escort from Redwood City to Federal Court beginning with pretrial motions.

When she came through the door into the booking room, I scarcely recognized her. The near-ragamuffin of September had given way to an attractively turned-out young lady in a well-tailored dark suit. The once-neglected nails had been trimmed and polished, her legs and armpits shaved. When I finished my shakedown by riffling through her hair, this time she paused to recomb it.

I felt a lot more sure of myself with my training behind me, and I think Patty sensed it. The search completed, I slipped the steel waist-chain around her—the four-foot chain goes on first, then one handcuff is inserted through its final loop, before the cuffs are fastened on the prisoner. That pretty much ties up the movement of the arms, preventing the prisoner from using the hand-cuffs like a hammer to bang somebody over the head.

Patty eyed me curiously. "Hey, that's a shiny set of handcuffs!"

"All my own." I adjusted them to the last notch. On Patty's skinny wrist, they still hung a bit loose.

"These are so stiff—and new!"

I grinned at her. "Don't worry, Patty. By the time I get through with you, they'll be old!"

Now we were both laughing. It's funny how most prisoners will help you along, once they get used to the idea of being handcuffed. They'll chirp out, "A bit tight there on the left" just as if they were being measured for a new suit.

I had begun calling her Patty as naturally as she used Janey, although later I found out that with other officers she insisted on being addressed as "Miss Hearst" or "Patricia." But we remained Patty and Janey except when, weeks afterward, we fell into the affectionate abusiveness common to good friends, greeting each other with "Weirdo," "Big Shit" and such. As we became closer, I think we both found the breezy, tough-guy manner a convenient shield against lapsing into a sentimentality that might get out of hand.

Still, I was cautious at the beginning, determined to steer a course between undisciplined fraternizing, which could be dangerous for both of us, and military

26

rigidity. "We're going to spend a lot of time together," I told her, "and regardless of how well we do or don't get along, we're going to have to make the best of it." I wanted her to know that this association wasn't going to be all fun and games. I had a job to do, and I'd appreciate her cooperation in helping me do it. In turn, I intended to be respectful of her dignity and integrity.

It didn't take us long to get down to what that meant, in terms of basic ground rules. I explained to Patty that any time we were in transit between protected areas, smoking was out of the question—for either of us. Lighted cigarettes, even in the friendliest of hands, are hazardous at close quarters. She would have to forego the cigarettes that were her constant ally against anxiety. "They make nasty burns," I pointed out. "I came into this job without any scars, and I intend to go out the same way."

It wasn't only for my protection, but for hers, too. "Suppose, suddenly, there's a gun on your right. What I have to do is knock you down. Instantly. I can't say to myself, 'Oh, I'm not able to knock you down because you have a cigarette in your hand. Put that cigarette out first.'

"There isn't going to be time to think about a cigarette. It's going to be 'Down!' and that's it."

Patty didn't argue. "Okay."

A couple of days later, Patty had to be taken from a holding cell at the back of marshal's headquarters down to the courtroom a floor below. That required handcuffs.

I found her—as usual—smoking.

"Put out the cigarette."

"Right."

"There's an ashtray over there." I pointed to the steel

bench running along the side of the cell.

Patty dropped her butt absently to the floor and ground her heel into it.

I felt it was necessary to establish who was in charge; and this was as good a time as any. "Okay, Patty. Pick up that cigarette and put it in the ashtray."

She looked at me disbelievingly. "You're kidding."

"No. That's why I told you there was an ashtray."

For just a split second she seemed to contemplate putting up a fight. Then she bent down and put the crushed cigarette where I had told her to.

A couple of hours later, there was a court recess, and Patty was sent to wait in an adjoining jury room. When the judge resumed proceedings, I was momentarily away in the rest room. One of the male deputies—my supervisor, actually—told Patty to get rid of her cigarette and come back to her attorneys' table.

Patty shook her head.

"Come on. What's the matter?"

"There's no ashtray."

"What are you talking about?"

"That lady marshal. She'll get really mad at me. Upstairs, she told me I had to use an ashtray."

Finally Patty was persuaded that it would be all right to stamp out her cigarette. But it didn't take long for word to get around the building that the awesome Patty Hearst, before whom everybody had been walking on eggshells, had been reined in by Janey Jimenez. I was summoned to my supervisor's office. "What did you do to her, Janey? She's afraid of you."

"That's good."

"No, it's not."

"Yes, it is. She knows who's in charge."

After that, Patty never balked at orders. She didn't even complain when I had to grab her suddenly—not always with ladylike gentleness—to move her away from possible danger.

If anything, she seemed more able to relax, as if she gained confidence from the feeling that I knew what I was doing. She started talking more on the rides to and from court: at first, about the meals at the Redwood City jail. Patty was a gourmet cook, a connoisseur of exotic dishes, and I gathered that the chef at the jail didn't quite come up to her standards. In fact, that had something to do with her continued loss of weight.

One evening, to her delight, I surprised her by turning over the unfinished half of my lunchtime chicken sandwich. That set her to chattering about the special pleasures of pheasant and duck.

Local duck, at a San Francisco restaurant?

"Oh no. Wild duck—from going out shooting with my father. When I was fifteen, he taught me how to shoot skeet."

Those treks through the marshes were great adventures, from Patty's description. "He'd get up at five in the morning, pull on his boots, and yank one of us out of bed to go with him. You never knew what day he'd pick, or where he might take you." There were trips with her father to San Simeon or other country places, fishing expeditions, long horseback rides in the hills. "The only thing you could be sure of was that you'd have a marvelous time."

By this point, I had read and heard all sorts of stories about Patty's supposed hostility to her parents. This didn't seem to fit the popular scuttlebutt at all.

From our chats over the next couple of weeks, before

the trial actually began, I was able to piece together a somewhat eye-opening picture of her relationship with her family.

To begin with, Patty wasn't particularly impressed with the exploits of her famous grandfather, William Randolph Hearst. I later learned that she had never read W. A. Swanberg's 1961 biography *Citizen Hearst* or seen Orson Welles' movie classic of twenty years earlier, *Citizen Kane*. She didn't enjoy being identified as the great man's granddaughter, but she didn't have any terrible hang-ups about it, either. Steven Weed, Patty's former fiancé, had claimed she found her name such a burden that she was thinking of changing it. But from everything she said, that idea never crossed her mind. The family name rang no bells with people, she told me, except for those connected with the Hearst enterprises.

She was vaguely aware that the old man had made a lot of money, and she was intrigued by those "little cemeteries for animals" he had scattered around San Simeon, because she was an animal-lover herself.

As for Patty contemplating suicide to escape the "burden" of her heritage, as intimated by a prosecution psychiatrist: hogwash. Even under extreme stress Patty has never had such leanings, as will become clear at a later point in my story.

On the other hand, Patty gave me plenty of reason to conclude that she enjoyed her family situation. Her father, in particular, came through from her accounts as a genial, easy-going man, not always predictable or consistent but always fun to be with. I got the impression that he was definitely the centerpiece of the family, adored by all of his five daughters, even though he changed his mind a lot.

Her feelings for her mother didn't seem quite as strong, or maybe more mixed. Mother was the one who insisted on sending her to strict Catholic schools, who was a stickler for the social proprieties. Yet when I showed her a snapshot of my mother, she commented with evident approval: "I like the way she holds herself—tall and erect. Like my mother." And she was proud of Catherine Hearst's wide knowledge of art.

My first actual contact with the Hearsts came during jury selection. Patty's parents looked pretty much as billed: Mrs. Hearst somber but controlled, her husband with his misery spilling out all over his face.

He first spoke to me in a whisper during a recess: "Do you go home with Patty—take her back to jail?" I nodded.

His next remark put me off a bit:

"Do you know if she's eating and sleeping all right?"

Without thinking, I ventilated my irritation: "I don't spend all *that* time with her—I have to have some life of my own!"

Later, I regretted the flip, almost nasty response. I hadn't realized the depth of the concern behind his question. It was months later before I fully realized his role in the family, when Patty was complaining about her sister Anne refusing to go to the hospital for a recommended check-up: "I told her that if she didn't go before I came home for Thanksgiving, I was going to tell Dad about it—and you know how Dad is. Dad will take her there, if he has to *carry* her to the doctor. . . ."

That was one tip-off. Earlier, the day before the jury verdict in the trial, there had been another. Since her capture by the FBI, Patty and her parents had had physical contact just twice: brief, awkward meetings in the

31

U.S. Marshal's San Francisco office and then at the Redwood City jail, both on the day of her arrest. All through the long, tortuous trial they had seen her only at a distance in the courtroom; and on their visits to the jail they had been separated by the bulletproof glass dividing the narrow little Visitors' Room, where communication was only by telephone.

With the verdict at hand, Judge Carter suddenly gave permission for Patty's parents and sisters to visit her in the unused courtroom next door. They filed in, one by one. Randy Hearst held out his arms and Patty ran to him. He hugged her, and she started bawling. Tears were welling up in his eyes, too.

Then she turned to her mother, and embraced Vicki and Anne, before reaching out to her father again. Everybody was weepy.

I could feel my own tears starting up. "C'mon, you guys. Cut it out. I can't handle this." Patty didn't stop crying, but from somewhere she smiled.

I can't believe that Patty Hearst was basically unhappy in her home life. It might have been less warm and zestful than those of more southern peoples; or less cohesive than is common among families who for economic reasons have to stay put. But what seems to me significant is that her memories of childhood—unlike my own—were essentially cheerful, affirmative. Never once, in all the spontaneous, impromptu comments I've heard fall from her lips has there been any kind of overt bitterness or even an unconscious "slip" indicating resentment of her family.

Then why did she never communicate with them, during seventeen months of wandering as a fugitive?

Deputy and prisoner emerge from San Mateo County Jail. "Painfully thin," handcuffs loose on her bony wrists, "Patty looked about as threatening as a baby rabbit."

When first assigned to guard Patty, Janey "had never carried a gun, much less fired one." Soon after, she was mastering the tear gas gun and .38 revolver at the Federal Law Enforcement Training Center in Glynco, Georgia.

"Shadow and companion, keeper and protector" of Patty for 350 hours.

UNITED STATES DEPARTMENT OF JUSTICE

FEDERAL BUREAU OF INVESTIGATION

WASHINGTON, D.C. 20535

April 19, 1974

RE: **DONALD DAVID DE FREEZE**
    NANCY LING PERRY

PATRICIA MICHELLE SOLTYSIK
CAMILLA CHRISTINE HALL

PATRICIA CAMPBELL HEARST
MATERIAL WITNESS

TO WHOM IT MAY CONCERN:

    The FBI is conducting an investigation to determine the whereabouts of these individuals whose descriptions and photographs appear below. Federal warrants charging robbery of a San Francisco bank on April 15, 1974, have been issued at San Francisco, California, for Camilla Hall, Donald DeFreeze, Nancy Perry, and Patricia Soltysik. A material witness warrant in this robbery has been issued for Patricia Hearst, who was abducted from her Berkeley, California, residence on February 4, 1974, by a group which has identified itself as the Symbionese Liberation Army (SLA). The participants in the bank robbery also claim to be members of the SLA.

DONALD DAVID DE FREEZE
N/M, DOB 11/16/43, 5'9" to 5'11",
150-160, blk hair, br eyes

PATRICIA MICHELLE SOLTYSIK
W/F, DOB 5/17/50, 5'3" to 5'4",
115, dk br hair, br eyes

PATRICIA CAMPBELL HEARST
W/F, DOB 2/20/54, 5'3", 110,
lt br hair, br eyes

MATERIAL WITNESS

NANCY LING PERRY
W/F, DOB 9/19/47, 5', 95-105, red
br hair, haz eyes

CAMILLA CHRISTINE HALL
W/F, DOB 3/24/45, 5'6", 125,
blonde hair, blue eyes

    If you have any information concerning these individuals, please notify your local FBI office, a telephone listing for which can be found on the first page of your directory. In view of the crimes for which these individuals are being sought, they should be considered armed and extremely dangerous, and no action should be taken which would endanger anyone's safety.

Very truly yours,

C. M. Kelley

Clarence M. Kelley

The FBI bulletin on fugitives sought for robbery of the Hibernia Bank. Against Patty's status of "most wanted," fledgling deputy Janey saw herself as "least qualified."

Wide World Photos

The Hearst jury: "a cross-section of middle America." But could laymen evaluate "psychological and medical complexities"? From left: Norman Grim, Robert K. Anderson, Stephen Riffel (alternate juror), Oscar McGregor, Jeri Jewitt (matron), William E. Wright (foreman), Cloveta Royall, Mary Nieman (alternate juror), Marilyn J. Wentz, Linda M. Magnani, Richard Ellis, Beatrice Bowman, Philip F. Crabbe, Bruce Braunstein, Marion P. Abe, and Chief Brophy.

Francis Lee Bailey — "direct, friendly, self-assured" — away from the defense table. Patty admired him deeply. But did his flamboyant courtroom tactics let her down?

J. Albert Johnson, Lee Bailey's not-so-silent partner. "Deeply concerned" about Patty, "this time . . . he intended to be noticed."

Co-council for defense J. Albert Johnson in playful moment with Janey. More often they wrangled. Janey felt he was "smothering" Patty with a super-protective attitude.

"Guarding Patty Hearst in San Francisco . . . was a nerve-wracking business." Around every corner might be lurking "some Lee Harvey Oswald with a high-powered rifle." Janey herself was the object of vicious threats.

Paul Sakuma

© *Chronicle Publishing Co., 1976*

Ordeal by camera: Patty and Janey run the gamut of newsmen and street crowds after court-ordered visit to Golden Gate Avenue apartment where Patty broke down after viewing her closet-prison.

"Roman holiday" or Greek tragedy? Unhappy Catherine Hearst outside courtroom with her husband. Despite "popular scuttlebutt" of discord between parents and daughter, Janey noted Patty's pride in her mother's art scholarship and regal carriage.

Paul Sakuma

United Press International Photo

Patty (center) "in battle regalia" covered by SLA gunwoman Nancy Ling Perry during Hibernia Bank robbery. Photo had "powerful negative impact" on jury. But "what was in her heart and mind at the time?"

For myself, I have to accept Patty's explanation—not just as delivered wearily and haltingly from the witness stand, but as elaborated on in a half-dozen private conversations with me.

For nineteen years she had been sheltered in the bosom of a wealthy family, insulated by her father from the harsh realities of life. He even financed her not-so-wild romantic fling with her fiancé, Steven Weed.

Then the SLA swooped down on her, totally shattering that delicate protective screen. Suddenly she was plunged into a world of rifle butts, naked force, wanton brutality.

Cut off from all familiar sources of support and information, she was told that she had been abandoned by her parents and friends; that despite their enormous power, nobody cared enough to make the necessary "modest" financial sacrifice.

After the Hibernia Bank holdup, a new note was added. The FBI, her captors said, was hunting her down like an animal. For confirmation, they showed her the assertion of the then U.S. Attorney General, William Saxbe, that she was no better than a "common criminal." She therefore had no choice, they told her, but to cast in her lot with them.

In her heart, Patty resisted this argument—until the day of the fiery SLA shoot-out with police in Los Angeles. Watching the battle over live TV, she had sat mesmerized while five hundred officers closed in on the hideout where, as the announcer repeatedly reminded his audience, Patty Hearst was "reported to be holed-up" with her revolutionary comrades. She saw the crouching police sharpshooters scuttle across the street before a wobbly hand-held camera; heard the crackle of rifle and automatic weapons fire; witnessed the crumbling of walls and finally the fierce blaze that soared up, enveloping the building and everyone within it. To her, the whole scene spoke of a determination to destroy, without any differentiation between willing and unwilling members of the insurgent gang. Looking at the charred ruins, in which she herself presumably lay, unmourned, she became convinced that, for whatever reason, she had indeed become an outcast from society.

At that point, I think, reality began slipping away from her. In her shrinking view of her predicament, nobody outside that burned-out house was trying to help her out or offer her refuge. The only exceptions, menacing though they might be, were the two surviving members of the SLA, Bill and Emily Harris. They were tangible, familiar, the sources of what little hope for security she still had. There was no choice but to run with them.

As she put it to me, "I felt that I had lost my parents, that they had once and for all turned away from me. Otherwise, how could they, with all the power and authority that the SLA kept insisting was at their command, have let this happen? Here was a building, supposedly with their daughter inside, being reduced to cinders, burned to the ground. And nobody was lifting a finger about it!

"Who was there to call, what was there to go home to, after that? I felt they had passed judgment on me.

"And then, that maybe they were right. I had gotten mixed into some terrible things—dragged in, but they didn't know that. Could I expect them to forgive me, to welcome me back after all the notoriety?

"Sure I loved my father and mother—and in a way, I

34

knew they loved me. But did they love me *that much*?"

To which I would add the comment of Jerri Jewett, the matron who was on hand the day that Patty and her parents were first brought together, a few hours after her arrest: "Patty was as happy at the meeting as they were. But—it's like she was more *scared*; timid, fearful of how she would be received . . . like a child who'd gotten lost and was half-expecting to be spanked for it."

In those early days of pretrial maneuvering, I saw a lot more of Patty's lawyers than of her parents. I liked Lee Bailey right away. He was direct, friendly, and self-assured, with a rich deep voice and an attractive smile. And he wore his courtroom laurels lightly, never seeming to need to push for attention or to put other people down.

I wasn't so sure about his less celebrated partner, J. Albert Johnson. As short as Bailey but conspicuously more pudgy (he became known around the courtroom as "Fat Albert"), Al Johnson showed an early taste for the limelight. I gathered that he felt the press had not been sufficiently appreciative of his past contribution to the success of the partnership, and that this time, at least, he intended to be noticed. He issued statements, managed to be seen frequently with the Hearsts, and generally made a point of throwing his considerable weight around.

To be fair, he did seem deeply concerned over Patty's plight. It was in their treatment of their client that the most marked difference showed up. Bailey had a wonderful way of kidding her, lightening the pressure of the moment by giving it a comic twist.

During a recess early in the trial, Patty asked to go to

the bathroom. "Okay, Janey," Bailey said genially, "take off her blindfolds"—a reference to the SLA practice of removing Patty's blindfolds only when she went to the bathroom.

Again, when Patty caught a respiratory infection and she and I both arrived wearing face masks, he quipped: "Perfect costume for a bank robber!" Bailey didn't encourage Patty to feel sorry for herself. He treated her like an adult: humanely, but without kid gloves.

Johnson, by contrast, usually wore an "Oh-the-pity-of-it" expression. No doubt this was partly out of genuine sympathy; but I had the feeling that he also enjoyed her dependency, gloried in the role of counselor-protector.

It was Johnson who charged out to buy Patty the proper courtroom-tailored clothes, who provided most of the coaching on how she should wear her hair, trim her nails, modulate her voice. He seemed determined to control every move she made. There was even a tendency to jostle aside anyone placed close to her by circumstances, like myself—as if he didn't want to share his prize.

This attitude of possessiveness beyond the call of duty bothered me; I wasn't at all sure that what Patty needed was more smothering. And I sensed possible trouble for myself in the vibes I was picking up from Al. I was right.

Guarding Patty Hearst in San Francisco, I discovered, was a nerve-wracking business. The city has a long tradition of gaudiness—and violence. The last ten years have been no exception. Kidnappings, bank robberies and a bomb-happy underground have created an atmosphere of terror, leading to extreme police countermeasures. Never more so than in the Hearst case, with its overflow of famous names, strong racial feelings, and explosive political issues.

Every step Patty took was protected by a living screen of deputy marshals, usually four to six strong. Checking out murder threats was a round-the-clock operation. Her schedule of movements was constantly varied to throw vengeance-seekers off the scent.

Patty's day began with a pick-up at the Redwood City jail somewhere between 5:30 and 7:00 A.M. I would already have been up for a couple of hours, traveling from my apartment in Daly City thirteen miles to the Marshals Service at the Federal Courthouse, then back down the San Jose freeway to get Patty. After the body-frisk for contraband, we would be taken by a security-tight elevator down to the basement "sally-port," where three cars would be waiting behind electronically controlled iron gates.

This was one of our maximum-danger spots. Coming out of the elevator, Patty and I had to take two or three steps in clear view of anyone across the lightly traveled street. Usually it was photographers who peered out from behind cottage doorways, parked cars, tree trunks. But it could just as easily be some Lee Harvey Oswald with a high-powered rifle. More than once, spotting an unfamiliar face, I had to slam Patty unceremoniously into our waiting car.

That was one of our rules—prisoners loaded first. I would get in alongside her, unarmed but covered by one of the two deputies up front. The idea was to discourage the prisoner from making a grab for the No. 1 guard's gun. So my .38, hidden in its custom-designed blue purse, rode in the trunk.

A third deputy, also armed, was at the wheel. Ahead of and behind us were marshals' vehicles with the back windows rolled down and shotguns at the ready.

Then came the forty-five-minute drive along the freeway, past low-rise apartments, motels, Candlestick Park, and the fog-shrouded Bay Bridge into downtown and the Federal Courthouse. Here another private elevator would whisk us up to the top floor, where Patty would be placed in a holding cell while I attended to other female prisoners. Then it was a controlled route, via secret, heavily guarded passageways, to the court-room.

The end of the day always brought another tense moment. Leaving from the security area two floors below street level, with the press, street mobs, and nobody could say who else waiting outside, our little caravan was preceded up the ramp by two deputies on foot,

38

carrying loaded shotguns. Not until the last minute, when Intelligence told us where the crowds were thickest, was the decision made whether to take the westward exit to Polk Street or the east to Larkin. Once, just to throw everybody off the track, we slipped out the main entrance directly onto Golden Gate Avenue.

Then came the return ride, an hour and a half in the late-afternoon traffic, to Redwood City; and for me, another wearying seesaw back to headquarters and then home. However if I had evening duty with the jury, my usual six or seven hours of sleep would be cut to three or less.

The jury assignment came up often because the panel (counting an alternate) included eight women, and it would not be in the interests of male deputies to be left alone with female jurors; there were too many possibilities for misunderstanding or false charges of impropriety. In a way I found the extra duty stimulating, opening up for me a wide range of interesting personalities.

One of my favorites was the jury foreman, a bluff, white-haired retired colonel in the Air Force named William Wright. Another was Bruce Braunstein, a quiet, thoughtful artist-type. With the youngest juror, Linda Magnani, I struck up an instant rapport. Linda was a pert receptionist who had just been married; although only twenty-four, she had a dry, ready wit. The older women talked to me about their families and treated me almost like a daughter.

But the job had its demanding side. Deputies had to make certain that no external influences intruded on the jurors' meditations; that they were kept bottled up in a private world where crime news was censored out of the newspapers and television viewing was restricted. Also, I had to be very careful to keep my two roles apart, never mentioning Patty to the jurors and vice versa. The upshot was quite a pileup of tension. One day when I was handling both Patty and the jury and was given the additional responsibility of escorting Sara Jane Moore, the would-be assassin of President Ford, I had to stay alert through 17½ hours of consecutive work.

But at least I had the freedom of my apartment, where I could take a glass of wine to help me fall asleep. Patty was under confinement every minute: in a bare 9 by 13 foot cell at Redwood City; in a bookless steel and concrete "holding tank" at the back of our office; in cars where she couldn't speak to a stranger or enjoy a soothing cup of coffee (on the premise that a hot liquid might be dashed into a guard officer's face). She couldn't even go to a rest room until it had been inspected for bombs. And she was on constant display before a voracious press.

I did what I could to make her situation livable. The message I conveyed was, "I'm in charge in this particular situation because this is my job, and there has to be some organized way of handling these things—but I have no thought of being above you as a person." I let her know that she had to respect me, but I didn't want to come across the way too many law-enforcement officers are seen by inmates: "me power-holder, you slave." What I said in effect was "We're two people caught in a situation; as long as you treat me humanly, I'll treat you humanly." And she responded in kind.

Several people have portrayed Patty as willful and stubborn, citing her rebelliousness at Santa Catalina, the Catholic girls' school she attended in Monterey. The difference is, I think, that there she was faced with authority exercised arbitrarily—a mindless "I outrank you, so do as I say." My experience was that if you gave her the reason for an order—took the trouble to explain the logic behind it—she always went along. Like with my command to douse her cigarette in the ashtray. Once she reflected on it for a moment she recognized that, surrounded as we were by potential menace, it was necessary for somebody to be consistently in charge.

I suspected she didn't relish the daily morning shakedown, so I tried to keep things light. "Hey, if you keep losing weight I'm not going to be able to tell your front from your back!"

Actually, she was painfully thin. Sometimes when I was taking off her waist-chain, the end would swing around and catch her in the pelvic area. The clank of steel against bone would make me wince. But Patty never complained.

It was easy to see why she wasn't putting back any weight. I caught a glimpse of her breakfast tray at the jail a few times, and it was really depressing: a kind of messy-looking gray mush without any flavoring, or cold fried eggs that looked as if they'd been sitting there for ten days. One decent roll and a cup of coffee, I thought to myself, would have made more sense for the same money.

In my occasional dealings with prisoners at MCC, supervising recreational areas and such, I had bent the rules before for inmates in uncomfortable situations, and I saw no reason to do less for Patty. Now and then, tucking a roll hastily into my purse as I left the house in the morning to make up for a missed breakfast, I would add an extra one for Patty. We would nibble together contentedly on our ride into the city, Patty bending over her handcuffs. And if time permitted, I might get another snack to her in the holding cell before the trial session began.

Our main food orgy—everything is relative—would come late in the afternoon, on the way back to Redwood City. Once I loaded my purse with popcorn, Coca-Cola, olives, and cake, and we had a real feast. Patty loosened up, handcuffs and all. Afterward, I lit a cigarette for her; she could get one out of the pack, but lighting it was tough.

The next morning, we clowned about the desirability of wrapping her up and shipping her to court in a mailbag, as had reportedly happened to a Mafia figure.

"No, thank you, Deputy! I've already had my experience along those lines!" She was referring to the time the SLA transported her in a garbage can.

"Deputy" was a term of endearment with her, reserved for the times when she thought I had said something kind of dumb. We were beginning to feel at home with each other. The contrasts between rich and poor, indulged and embattled, were falling away; now we were relating as two women in their early twenties.

Young people today have more in common than just blue jeans and a freer vocabulary. Like Patty, I grew up in the America of the 1960s. Whereas my mother felt strongly the sting of class, and was always worrying about "doing the right thing," for my generation it was doing your *own* thing that counted.

Money didn't matter. The school I went to in Van Nuys had kids from the movie world, like the sons of Steve Allen and Dick Van Dyke, and from wealthy Jewish families. We all swapped overnight visits, although I could put up a guest in our two-bedroom home only if one of my four sisters slept elsewhere. At the Jimenez house you had to make your own breakfast; invitations to me provided a private room, sometimes with a maid in attendance.

Patty and I both saw people as individuals, and that was always in the background of our relationship. I never pushed her for confidences, or asked anything that I thought she might be reluctant to tell me. In fact, I made a point of saying, "Patty, if you ever feel I'm bringing up something that's none of my business, say so." It never happened.

I even held off from the usual commiserations: "I'm so sorry for you. . . . I know what you've been through." *Nobody* could know, who hadn't experienced her particular terror. It would have been phony to pretend that I could imagine something beyond my imagining. To be suddenly ripped away from your family—sexually brutalized—forced to play the criminal—it was more than my head could cope with.

And it was not only the events themselves that no one could share with Patty; even more, it was what they meant to her, how they were processed in her mind.

So when she occasionally complained, "I was raped in that closet. Can't they understand that?" I confined myself to a "Hang in there, Patty," and a pat on the back.

The day-to-day pressures on her were something else. I understood them, could see what it was like to be constantly under surveillance, and had enough sense to leave her alone when she didn't want to talk.

When the chance came to make a harmless friendly gesture, I didn't get hung up on regulations. For instance, early in the trial she was given a pair of birthday rings by her sister Anne, simple ivory bands of elegant design. They were the first jewelry Patty had had in many months, and she wore them proudly in court, together on the fourth finger of her right hand.

But prisoners were not allowed to have jewelry in their cells, on the premise that it could be traded for weapons or drugs, or used for self-injury. So every evening at the end of the court session I removed the rings from Patty's finger, put them in a pink box, and returned them to her the next morning.

Our growing intimacy was not taken kindly by most of my fellow-deputies. One of the exceptions was Glen E. Robinson, supervisor of the Criminal Department and my immediate supervisor. The first black deputy in the Northern District of California, commanding a staff of thirty-one, Glen had bucked his way up the hard way; he needed no spelling out in capital letters of my vulnerable position as a young minority-female. Glen was married and the father of three lively children. Like the man over both of us, Chief Deputy Brophy, he was unfailingly supportive.

Not so his colleagues. They lost no opportunity to criticize my tactics, ridicule my considerateness for Patty, and get in a dig or two on a more personal level.

After we had made the run between jail and courthouse a few times, I mentioned to Patty that I lived along the route, and pointed out the apartment building just off the freeway in Daly City. The other deputies were scandalized. How could I tell a suspected revolutionary, who probably still had ties with the underground, where I could be found alone at night? Didn't I realize I was setting myself up for assassination? They had never heard anything so naive, etc., etc.

It was a couple of days before I got over that one.

They were always ribbing me about being too close to my prisoner. One day I came in wearing a jumpsuit lettered "Montreal, '76," but the letters were obscured by my coat. The deputy at the next desk peered over at me: "What does that say—'Free Patty'?"

Then there was the below-the-belt stuff, directed at my sex ("Not bad for a female") and, more irritatingly, at my Mexican ancestry. Somebody would twirl the knobs of the car radio for a Spanish-language broadcast, call it loudly to my attention ("This is for Janey, folks") and then proceed to make fun of it. Or suggest that at the next rest-station stop, we get some *burritos* or *tacitos* "for Janey's sake—after all, it'll be May 5 in a couple of months." *Cinco de Mayo* is the Mexican national holiday celebrating the victory of Juarez over the invading French at Puebla in 1867.

That's when Patty would jump in, sharply: "All right, you guys, lay off her! Leave Janey alone!"

Behind the not-so-good-natured gibes was the fact that a lot of these fellows had been around for years without getting any attention while I, a callow recruit, had my picture splashed all over the papers on my very first day on the job. A female deputy marshal was a novelty; such assignments had always been handled on a fill-in basis by matrons or secretaries.

More than that, everything connected with the Hearst case was gobbled up by the media. Their relentless attentions were very trying for Patty. It seemed to me that some reporters had, so to speak, smelled the blood from her wounds, and were bent on making a feast for themselves of her feelings. To me that was as barbarous as consuming her flesh. Patty herself saw a parallel with the media treatment accorded to the late blues singer Billie Holiday, whose tragic misadventures were chronicled in pitiless detail.

Still, I can't put all the blame on those who were covering the story. Behind them were undoubtedly a great many people seeking escape from their own family problems. According to a recent study, the suicide rate among Americans aged fifteen to twenty-four has more than doubled in the past twenty years. I'm sure there were readers and viewers who, unable to manage their own lives and particularly their children, took pleasure in the troubles of the famous.

Some of the build-up by the rival TV and news services was ridiculous, to the point where when Patty needed a haircut, a special court order was required. And when I was caught up momentarily in the exhaust draft from a helicopter, the story went out that I had been all but decapitated.

The media were a problem—and to make the problem endurable, we turned it into a game. Patty, under standing instructions from Al Johnson, was never to let a photographer get a picture of her smiling; he was afraid people would think she was frivolous, taking her trial like a lark.

So at the close of every session, as we descended by special elevator toward the media people waiting in the basement, I would urge her to "Put on an Unhappy Face." It might take five or ten seconds, if she was in a good mood, to work up the required solemn pose.

Once I asked if she wouldn't like to forget Johnson's theory, and come out as her natural self.

"You mean like this?" She leaped out toward an

46

imaginary camera, flung her arms wide apart, and flashed a dazzling smile. I hardly recognized my glum prisoner.

But that was a private show. With the photographers, who were always trying to get a rise out of her, she was stubbornly resolved to stand her ground. On her birthday, February 20, they did everything but handsprings to provoke a reaction. But Patty held firm.

As I joined her in the car, she turned to me proudly: "They didn't get a thing."

Still, the press coverage piled up—including TV footage on me and features in such publications as *Newsweek* and *People*, along with lots of photos. At twenty-three, without raising a finger for it, I was acquiring a fat scrapbook. The other deputies didn't like it.

Ugly rumors began circulating, to the effect that I was being paid off by the Hearsts. I make a point of dressing carefully; I work hard for my money, and I figure I'm entitled to. One morning I came in wearing a combination of a red cashmere sweater and a gray flannel skirt. My partner on the shift stared meaningly: "Hey, that's quite an outfit! Did Randy give it to you?"

They went further. I found a note on my desk summoning me to the big boss of the Northern California district, U.S. Marshal Frank Klein. Frank is a plump, friendly man, usually pouring out a stream of bad jokes. But this day he was very serious.

"Tell me, Janey—have you accepted anything from the Hearst family—a gift, a sandwich, even a stick of gum? Have they bought you a drink after work, has anybody seen you with them?"

I shook my head.

"Think hard. Have they given you anything at all?"

"No, they haven't. Why—are they *going* to give me something?"

Frank broke into a smile. Obviously, whatever he had heard, this particular deputy wasn't on the take. "Forget it, Janey. We don't have to talk about it any more."

The ironic fact was that for all their innuendoes and their complaints about my being a publicity hound, the other deputies fought like cats for the assignment to join me in escorting Patty back to Redwood City every evening, since it meant a sure-fire picture in the paper. One minute they would be twitting me—"Boy, I wish *I* was being interviewed every day to tell the world what color eye shadow I wear"—the next they would be lining up before my superiors, hollering, "I haven't had my turn yet!"

I could usually count on the second deputy to contribute a shove or two when we got out of the elevator, literally elbowing me out of the way to make certain his face was within camera range.

Finally I went back to Marshal Klein: "Look, they can *have* their pictures on the front page. I'm not interested in a publicity contest. But I won't stand for any more of this hauling and shoving!" The day before, when I was delayed by a rip in my skirt, they had actually tried to take off without me. I had to throw myself into the car to avoid being left behind.

Patty's parents, too, got a lot of attention from the media. The Hearsts were in faithful attendance at the trial every morning, always in the same drab outfits of black or banker's gray. I was intrigued by the modesty of their wardrobes. As I remarked to Glen Robinson, "I guess when you have that much money, it doesn't matter how you dress. The rest of us try to put the best foot

48

forward. They don't have anybody to impress."

The Hearsts were pathetically eager to communicate with their daughter. In court, they framed silent little messages of encouragement with their mouths until I warned them that reporters were reading their lips. Because of constant threats against their lives, they were allowed to come up from the basement garage via the judges' elevator, and proceed by a private corridor directly to their seats. One time they emerged from the elevator just as Patty and I were coming from the direction of the judges' chambers, and I wanted to let parents and daughter have a brief word together; but Patty, not seeing them, had already turned the corner.

She was really shattered when, late in the trial, her father was called to the witness stand: "People think I didn't want to see my father. I wanted to see him so badly . . . but not up there on that stand." And the next day, when her mother was photographed in tears after testifying: "How could they do that to her? Of course I want to see my mother—but not a picture of her in the newspaper, blowing her nose!"

5

The huge gray Federal Building in San Francisco spreads an air of judicial majesty over a square city block. It has a wide landscaped plaza and a marble lobby, with modern-art decor, three stories high. On its twentieth and top floor, commanding a sweeping view of the Civic Center to the south, are the headquarters of the Marshals Service, where I had a desk and a private locker.

Patty's trial was held one flight below, in a spacious ceremonial courtroom usually reserved for committee hearings of the United States Congress or the swearing-in of new judges. Some 60 feet long and 50 feet wide, with a skyscraper ceiling, it had a broad podium at the far end for the judge's bench.

From the main entrance, the jury box was on the right. Directly across was a similar box for the press, whose ninety-odd members also spilled over into adjacent seats. Tables for the prosecution and defense staffs ran at right angles to the judge, with the government attorneys seated on the side closer to the jury. The witness stand was at the judge's left, on a diagonal about halfway between him and the jury.

Patty sat at the defense table, usually between Lee

Bailey, farthest down front, and Al Johnson. Her parents and other Hearsts were a few feet away in the first row of the spectators' section, with her father always in the aisle seat. I sat, flanked by another deputy, directly behind Patty.

Security precautions were prodigious. Courtroom, judge's chambers, jury room and nearby quarters were scoured for bombs before each session. Deputies stationed outside the courtroom screened all arrivals for weaponry with an airport-type machine. And twelve to fifteen deputies were on constant patrol inside, alerting each other by walkie-talkie to possible sources of trouble.

It wasn't only the Hearsts who were getting threats. Every day brought hate mail and vicious calls directed at me.

The letters were relayed to the FBI, who checked them out before turning them over to Marshal Klein. I saw a few of them, one from a girl who was quite emphatic about wanting to see me six feet under.

The calls were put through to the Sheriff's Department. The most persistent caller was a man who asserted I was a whore picked up from the streets and that I was being so nice to Patty because I was probably in on the whole anti-Establishment conspiracy. As a member of a minority group, he pointed out helpfully, I would no doubt have my own reasons for joining the disaffected circle of the SLA. It was not comforting to realize that this man was on the loose in San Francisco, possibly within gun or knife range at any moment.

On Thursday evening, February 19, a half hour before I was to go off guard duty with the jurors at midnight, a call came in to the deputies' room at the Holiday Inn from the Sheriff's Department: an assassin was going to "get Patty Hearst" on her way to court the next morning, Patty's birthday.

Glen Robinson walked with me out to my car. The warning having just come in, he thought "some lunatic" might already be waiting outside the hotel. He wanted to be sure I had my .38 with me: "Take it out of your purse and put it in your pocket. And call me the minute you get home, to say you're okay."

The next morning, there were no government cars escorting Patty to and from the courthouse. Our whole group traveled in unmarked private vehicles, and we took a completely new route. Patty wondered why.

"We wanted to make it special for your birthday," I explained. She looked skeptical, but didn't press the point.

Court started promptly every morning at 9:30, with Judge Oliver J. Carter breaking for recesses around 10:45 and again in mid-afternoon. In the six weeks of testimony, there were long, dry stretches where Patty and I, up since dawn, had trouble keeping our eyes open. We would fight off sleep by exchanging amused glances toward others apparently in the same predicament—especially Judge Carter, who frequently leaned back as if dozing. But lawyers who tried to slip anything past him soon discovered he was quite awake.

The recesses were a great relief: an occasion for rest room and chats, and for diverting ourselves by taking pot shots at various courtroom figures. We settled early on our first target: the earnest, lanky chief prosecutor, U.S. Attorney James L. Browning. Browning had fumbling ways in court. He was apt to trip, à la Gerald Ford, over the huge exhibit charts he carried around, such as the diagram of the Hibernia Bank lobby; and he couldn't always keep dates and names straight.

As administrator of the government legal staff for a large federal district, Browning had not personally tried a major court case for five years. Perhaps for that reason, his technique in cross-examination tended to be laborious. When Patty took the stand on February 9, the fourth day of the trial, he questioned her persistently about her failure to have bowel movements when the SLA first locked her in a closet. Didn't they ever let her out? Weren't bathroom facilities provided? Then how come—?

"I should have told him," Patty commented to me drily during the next recess, "that I was scared shitless."

On February 20, Patty was able to register a private triumph over the prosecutor. A week earlier, a bomb had blasted open a wall at Hearst Castle, causing a million dollars in damages to furniture and art objects. Responsibility was soon claimed by a radical underground group, the New World Liberation Front.

But the jury, cut off from press reports and the outside world generally, knew nothing about the incident—until Browning arranged for Patty to tell them.

She was back on the stand. The U.S. attorney, in his plodding, persistent way, was badgering her over the fact that during two long cross-country journeys she had never attempted to notify the police where they could get their hands on the Harrises.

"There were many other people," Patty responded, "that could have picked up where they [the Harrises] left off and if they'd wanted me dead, all they had to do is say that's what they'd want."

What ever made her believe that, once in police custody, the Harrises could still "have you turn around and have you killed?"

"It's happening like that now on the street."

"What do you mean, Miss Hearst?" The question popped out like an exploding champagne cork. Browning tried to snatch it back, or at least reshape it to "Has somebody been killed?" but Judge Carter wasn't having any. He ruled that Patty was entitled to answer the original question.

"Well," she said with great relish, "San Simeon was bombed, my parents received a letter threatening my life . . . their lives if I took the witness stand; and they wanted a quarter of a million dollars put into the Bill and Emily Harris defense fund."

Who did? The New World Liberation Front. So, into the record—and the ears of the jurors—went the evidence of continuing terrorist threats against the Hearsts. At the time, it seemed hard to believe it would not weigh heavily in their verdict. Coming down from the stand, Patty was almost jubilant. At recess, she told me: "Browning couldn't have given me a better birthday present."

Browning, of course, was very conscious of his blunder. That evening he came up to me in the Rathskeller, a popular restaurant across the street from the courthouse. It was clear that he had already been to the bar. What was he doing wrong? he demanded. "You know the jury, Janey—you work with them. Should I be using some other approach?"

I reminded him that this kind of questioning was out of bounds, and he retreated apologetically. But the incident underlined for me how much was at stake for him in the trial.

Patty too was aware of his bulldog determination to win, and she resented it. She thought Browning was smug and insensitive. Driving to the hospital for skull x-rays, to establish that she had indeed been bludgeoned by the SLA, she commented: "People like Browning think I actually went along on purpose with the SLA, that I'm still with them. Let people like that, just once, go around and see what it feels like to get hit in the head. It leaves a scar, all right—not only on your skull, but inside!"

Browning reminded her, Patty once said, of her former fiancé, Steven Weed. I think she was referring to the prosecutor's know-it-all manner.

Other targets for Patty's backstage comment were the two progovernment psychiatrists, Drs. Joel Fort and Harry L. Kozol. She called Kozol "the little bug," and did a hilarious imitation of his pinched, whiny voice. Patty was a sharp observer of other people's traits, an excellent mimic—something to remember in appraising her apparent accommodation to the SLA.

Late in February, Patty noticed a ring on my left hand, a pink star sapphire with four small diamonds.

"Hey, that's a real knockout," she said. "Where did you get it?"

"From a guy I almost married—but didn't."

"That sounds familiar. You know, I once had this beautiful opal that Steven Weed gave me. I thought that if we got married, it would be my wedding ring."

"I had the same idea."

"Why didn't you get married?"

"I don't know . . . I was getting a different outlook on

55

life, wanted a little more time. I felt that if he loved me, he'd accept that. But—I guess he didn't."

Patty gave me a strange look. "How old were you?"

"Seventeen."

"And your boyfriend?"

"Oh, he was in his early twenties."

"That's amazing." Patty fell silent.

"Why?"

"Because Steven and I were almost exactly the same distance apart."

That fact seemed to create a bridge for Patty, a thin edge of security along which she could extend her trust. She started to tell me about Steven Weed, how she had half-drifted into the relationship because he was an "older man," sophisticated, former captain of the Princeton track team.

I knew what she was talking about. Having lost my father under bitter circumstances at thirteen, I had been in search of a protective older figure myself. "It's like having a father all your own," I suggested. "There all the time."

We seemed to have gone down very much the same road. You're restless living at home, or at school away from home, and you meet someone who's attractive. You say to yourself, "Now I don't need my family; I've got him. I can be independent, lead my own life." But that can be an illusion. You may remain as dependent as ever.

As Patty put it: "You grow up with this person, and he teaches you all kinds of things, and you love him. But what you don't realize is that in effect you're still living with Daddy. You've just changed your address.

"Till one day you see some other kinds of people,

56

and—well, that may not be a better situation but you don't know whether it's better or not. You want to have the experience for yourself before you make a commitment."

We were both frankly confused on the subject of love. "You can love someone—or *think* you love him—at the moment you're with him," Patty went on, "and then move into a new environment, different surroundings, and find he doesn't look the same to you. You might even ask yourself, 'Did I really ever love that person?' And you have to remind yourself, 'Yes, you did. But in a different time and place.'"

I confessed that I was still muddled about my boyfriend: "I really don't know this minute if I do love him, or hate him. I feel that I never want to see him again—and yet I know that I do want to."

Patty nodded. "I guess I feel the same way about Steven."

Months later, I took a stroll through the student-residence area in Berkeley where Patty had lived with Steven Weed, eight blocks south of the University of California campus. Although Patty never mentioned it, the campus was dotted with landmarks bearing her family name: Hearst Field, Hearst Gymnasium, Hearst Greek Theater.

The atmosphere along Telegraph Avenue, the local Main Street, was casual, friendly and a little freaky—full of sidewalk pottery stands, lady snake charmers, *felafel* restaurants and African curio shops—the perfect setting for a cosy, parent-financed college romance. But not for a lifetime commitment. I could see where it might have been wearing thin for Patty.

Incidentally, the district struck me as completely

harmless. The nearest thing in sight to revolutionary fanaticism was a small hand-printed sign, "Boycott grapes."

I don't think Patty's feelings about Steven Weed really crystallized, at least for the moment, until he started working on his book. She was still in jail when he was scurrying around trying to track down letters they had exchanged. Patty was indignant: "How can he expose my personal life like that? I think it's despicable."

Then, just before his scheduled trial appearance as a witness on her behalf, Weed gave a press conference. Patty's lawyers were incredulous; they decided not to have him testify.

The book itself drew more angry comment from Patty: "Even the pictures that he claims are his were mine, taken with my camera! And he's still hanging on to china, personal gifts from my grandmother, meaningless to him. . . ."

Her final blast was over Weed's reaction to the SLA kidnappers who burst into their apartment. As Weed reported it in his book, he said "Take anything you want and leave us alone." Patty's version was, "and leave me alone." She interpreted that as an invitation to the SLA to carry her off.

"If you really love someone," she stormed, "how can you say, 'Take anything, but leave me alone!' So they took me."

Patty's sexual attitudes had a direct bearing on the bank robbery charges against her. There was no debate about her participation in the holdup. The heart of the government's case lay in the claim that she had acted voluntarily, as a convinced and even enthusiastic member of the SLA—"a queen in the army," as psychiatrist Joel Fort testified. Prosecutor Browning leaned heavily on the argument of Dr. Fort and Dr. Harry Kozol that Patty was a sexual and social rebel from adolescence—no longer a virgin at fifteen, angry at her parents, defiant of all authority, "ripe for the plucking" when the SLA grabbed her.

They connected her alleged receptiveness to a kind of disease of American youth, especially in the pampered upper middle class, to which most of her captors belonged. And they insinuated that captors and captive alike had a taste for thrill-seeking which, combined with "racial guilts," would make an affair with a black convict like the SLA's "General Field Marshal" Cinque attractive.

According to Browning's experts, her protests of an initial rape by Willie Wolfe were a sham. Actually, Kozol insisted, she gave every sign of having been deeply involved with Wolfe.

Well, what did I learn of Patty's sexual viewpoints that could throw some light on the likelihood of such a romance, and on the chances of her being impressed by Cinque?

Plenty. Patty and I talked a lot about our role as females, the way any two women of our ages might. Our conversations ranged over all sorts of sexual issues: how we felt about marriage, fidelity, physical versus emotional involvement, feminism. And we often whiled away stretches of boredom on long automobile rides by comparing notes on the passing male scene as visible from our windows.

Our basic attitudes turned out to be remarkably similar. For instance, we agreed that women should have equal opportunities with men for jobs and education; Patty wouldn't let the male deputies get away with raw gibes against me. Not that she ever got on a soapbox about it; she simply knew where she stood, and took a firm stand. She also felt that women should be as free as men to take the initiative socially, rather than have to wait to be asked.

But that was it. Neither of us had any sympathy for the extremist "Who needs men?" pose, that sneers at small courtesies like having a door opened for you. I don't mind playing a slightly subordinate role sexually. And I think Patty takes the same view.

Essentially, she likes to feel feminine. And she has an appealing femininity. She isn't a striking beauty, like her mother or her older sister Gina; her features are not particularly memorable. Yet there is a mischievous quality to her smile, a lilt in her walk, and a breeziness in her conversation that make her good company. Patty knows how to handle herself with men: when to be suitably crushing with a man on the make, when and how to turn him away without wrecking his ego.

With all this, there is also a distinctly intellectual side to her make-up, that only a brainy man would appreciate. She seems to crave verbal contact—intense discussions, humorous exchanges—in a word, companionship. It's the full content of a relationship that's important to her.

Once during the trial I complained about how the day and night grind was crippling my social life. Patty agreed—but not in terms of being "horny," deprived of sensual experience. What bothered her was not having a man around she could talk to.

Casual touching doesn't mean a thing to her; if anything, she dislikes it. The touching has to be by someone she cares about, and who has demonstrated a concern for her. Cats take pleasure in being stroked; they'll brush up against you just for the pure sensual delight of it. Not Patty. She's an affectionate person, but sexual contact has to be personal, special, meaningful. She could never fling her body around promiscuously, or give herself carelessly to just anybody.

That basic choosiness, almost primness, was evident every time she was the object of a wolfish approach. Once, as she was getting into the car, one of the deputies remarked, "Boy, you sure have nice pins!"

"What's *that*?" Patty asked flatly.

"You know—legs. I wonder what they're like a little higher."

"Take a good look now, Buster. That's all you're ever going to see."

Another would-be Romeo objected that he never saw Patty except with handcuffs on: "How do you look with them off?"

"You'll never know."

On some days the in-transit boredom was so desperate that, to pass the time, we would stare out the window at passing cars and jokingly tick off our preferences as to male riders and passengers. The deputies noticed our game and deliberately teased us, slowing down whenever they passed a good-looking girl but speeding up when we spotted a man.

Patty's choices astonished me. She would invariably go for some square-jawed, neatly-dressed character right out of an old Arrow Collar ad, the very opposite of shaggy, rumpled types like Steven Weed. My tastes were more offbeat, and Patty in turn professed to be

61

baffled by them. Once we were stuck at a traffic-light alongside a really fat, slovenly little man. Patty nudged me, winking: "There's your boy, Janey. Go get him!"

Her own favorite was a deputy who had served with us for ten days in February until he left to join the Secret Service. He was husky, articulate, not too far-out but definitely with-it . . . a perfect Mr. Straight, buttressed by depth.

The conventional tone of her approach to sex was underlined in a talk we had after her conviction. She had never mentioned lesbian practices in the SLA, at least two of whose women members were involved in an intense relationship. But now, facing a prison term, she was terrified at the prospect of being approached by a homosexual inmate. "How could anyone be that way? If they ever came near me—ugh!"

Patty's face reflected her extreme revulsion.

This attitude, spontaneously expressed and obviously felt down to the marrow, did not square with the radical feminism attributed to Patty by the government lawyers and in fact parroted by Patty herself immediately after her arrest. The prosecution made much of the crusading women's lib literature found in the apartment she shared with Wendy Yoshimura, and of the notes in Patty's handwriting on sexism and women's rights.

All I can say is that if she was a dedicated, militant feminist, she certainly changed fast. It's been my observation that women so committed are not shy about letting the world know it. And Patty simply didn't, in all the time I have known her, carry this chip on her shoulder. I would have to conclude that the feminist books and the note-scribbling were indeed, as Patty claims, part of her act to convince her captors that she was a loyal SLA "soldier."

Willie Wolfe was the son of a divorced Pennsylvania physician. A gangling, freckle-faced 22-year-old, he and Bill Harris were the two whites who along with Cinque (formally, Donald DeFreeze) made up the male contingent of the kidnap gang. There were also five women, all white. Early in the trial, Patty testified that she had been sexually assaulted by Wolfe, and subsequently by Cinque.

According to her account, after weeks of being shut up and blindfolded in a narrow closet, she had a visit there from Angela Atwood, the ex-school teacher from New Jersey who with Cinque and Harris had allegedly carried out the actual kidnapping. Atwood told her that since she was living within an underground cell, she would have to become familiar with the SLA code. It was customary for members of the group to fill each other's sexual needs; she had been chosen to serve as Willie Wolfe's partner.

That same night, Patty said, Wolfe came to her in the closet and told her to lie down. Fearful for her life, she testified, she did not resist.

Months later, after Wolfe had been killed in the SLA shoot-out in Los Angeles, he was eulogized by Patty in a tape recording, the third and last of the "Tania" messages delivered in her ostensible new role as a dedicated member of the underground. The tape spoke of her imperishable love for "Cujo"—Wolfe's code name in the SLA—"the gentlest, most beautiful man I've ever known. . . . Neither Cujo nor I had ever loved an individual the way we loved each other, probably because our relationship wasn't based on bourgeois, fucked-up values."

At her trial, Patty disclaimed responsibility for all her taped messages, saying they were dictated by her captors or composed and recorded under the threat of death.

But the proprosecution psychiatrist Harry Kozol insisted that the references to Willie Wolfe were spoken by Patty "so lovingly and so tenderly and so movingly" as to persuade him otherwise. Furthermore, said Kozol, when he questioned her in jail about her feelings for Wolfe, "she seemed to get upset and deeply moved. I felt that she was almost sobbing inside."

When Patty took the stand for cross-examination, prosecutor Browning pursued the same line:

"Did you, in fact, have a strong feeling for Cujo?"

"In a way, yes."

"As a matter of fact, did you love him?"

"No."

Nor, she said firmly, did she "develop a certain affinity" for Willie Wolfe, as suggested by Browning.

What then was the "strong feeling" to which she referred?

"I couldn't stand him."

As court recessed for the day a few minutes later, I could see that Patty was very tense. Going back upstairs to the Marshals Service, she seemed eager to talk. But we were surrounded by male deputies with their ears standing up, obviously bursting with curiosity; so I signaled her to wait.

Driving back in the car, she poured out her feelings: "What do you do when someone comes in, and you're wearing blindfolds, and you don't even know who it is?

64

When somebody comes into a closet and just says—just gets on top of you—what do you do? Are you going to—if you refuse, are you going to be alive tomorrow? And even if you *do* do it, does that mean you'll be allowed to live afterward?"

In a half-dozen later references by Patty to Willie Wolfe, I never heard any hints of emotional involvement, sentiment, or even passionately negative feelings: only a kind of detached disgust.

More impressive than any words was Patty's reaction on a court-ordered inspection visit, made for the benefit of the jury, to the two stuffy windowless closets where she had been held. The first, in suburban Daly City, was a little over two feet deep and six feet seven inches wide; the second, in San Francisco, was even more constricted: 18 inches by five feet nine. For some 57 days she was crammed into these narrow cubicles—her eyes covered, the click of gunbolts and the sound of mocking voices coming to her ears. Perhaps the worst torment, as she portrayed it to me, was the noisy thumping of rock broadcasts turned on by the SLA to mask their conversations. She found it disturbing, disorienting, a sea of sound that made a hodgepodge of time and place. As she said, "With your eyes covered and your ears drowning in noise, you have no contact with the outside. You feel cut off, helpless. Just your head is left, to imagine." In her original affidavit filed when applying for bail, Patty spoke of only one closet. I think in her mind the two consecutive confinements were blurred into a single harrowing experience in which she was slammed away, as she put it to an interviewing psychiatrist, "like a *thing*."

65

For the site-viewing during the trial, we went first not to the initial hideout in Daly City but to the shabby third-floor apartment on Golden Gate Avenue where Patty was taken some time around mid-March. When Patty and I arrived with several other deputies the busload of jurors were still in transit. But the media were already assembled in full force; a swinging television camera hit me in the eye.

We went upstairs, and for a few minutes sat in the kitchen at the back of the apartment. Patty was visibly jumpy. Two men from the prosecutor's staff came in, snooping around to see how she was taking the visit. Al Johnson joined us, and then we heard the jurors approaching.

Al told Patty to stand in the doorway, so the jurors could get a good close-up look at her as they filed past into the studio-living room; even on the witness stand, she had been at least five feet away from them.

I objected, pointing out that the doorway was open to a potential line of fire through the double bay windows that looked out onto the street. But Al waved me away, and the jury moved past Patty as she stood there, half-sniffling into a Kleenex.

The jurors shuffled over to the closet, peered in, and filed their way back again. The only one who displayed any response was Mary Nieman, an alternate; she exclaimed, "Oh, my God!"

When they had gone, Al went into the living-bedroom and motioned to Patty: "Hon, I want you to come over and look at this closet."

"She'll be too close to those windows, Al," I protested.

He gave no indication of hearing me. Patty looked at

him pleadingly, obviously shaky and hesitant.

"Come on," he repeated. "Come on."

I don't know why he was so insistent; perhaps because Patty was due to resume testifying the next day, and he thought the reminder would intensify her emotionality on the stand. Personally, I found the maneuver heartless, whatever his motive.

Very slowly, Patty moved toward the closet. The door was open. She fixed her gaze inside for an instant, then turned away.

"No no," said Al impatiently. "I want you to take a really good long look at it."

Like an obedient child, she did as she was told.

"Is that the way it was?"

"Yes."

"Okay, I want you to think about that, and remember it. . . ."

Patty turned back. A look was spreading over her face, a look of helplessness and despair, and of something like retreat, departure. It was as if she were going off into another world. I had seen that look before, on epileptics just before going into an attack.

And on Patty herself, in a different time and place: when she lay writhing on the gynecological examining table at Stanford Hospital.

In my mind, there was and is no question that at that moment, in the bare and dreary Golden Gate Avenue apartment, she was in headlong flight from the memory of Willie Wolfe's visits, fighting off horrors too fresh to recall.

Seconds later, just as at the hospital, she exploded into uncontrollable tears.

But by the time we emerged into the hallway of the

building, she had reduced the weeping to a few sniffles. People in the neighboring apartments had come out to wave and wish her luck. Patty raised her eyes, managed a "thank you" and put her head down again.

The mask was restored, her emotions brought under control—perhaps, I suspect, at the ultimate cost of her legal freedom. For this recurring evaporation of expression, this automatic cut-off of feelings to preserve her sanity, must have left judge and jurors baffled. More than a year would pass before several of the jurors would, stirred by their own intervening experiences, come to see Patty's remoteness in a new and more sympathetic perspective.

If the "grand romance" theory about Willie Wolfe seems a dubious proposition, the notion of Patty welcoming Cinque as a lover raises even more serious doubts. Black sexuality on the California scene was something on which she had firm and long-standing views, views which I fully shared.

I don't make a habit of tossing around racial generalizations lightly; as an American of non-*anglo* background, I'm in no position to. And it would be against my most deeply held convictions, anyway. I don't feel that any group has a monopoly on virtues—or vices. For the economic and cultural deprivation imposed on blacks, as on other minorities, I have nothing but indignation.

But I can't blink at certain facts of my experience. And from our conversations it was clear that it was an experience shared with Patty.

We've both found that within the specific environment of our West Coast campuses, the part of the world we know best—and I'm not extending this to other times, places, or age groups—young black men come on awfully strong, to the point of being a distasteful turn-off. Whether it's because they've been spoiled by sensation-seeking white girls, are making up for the putdowns they're subjected to in our society, are taking seriously the popular myth about supposed black virility, or there is some other explanation, I can't say; but some of them are just plain arrogant. It doesn't matter whether they're handsome or ugly. They just crook a finger and expect a girl to fall over.

Mexican or Hispanic men, by contrast, will make the same pitch but display some finesse about it. The black studs I'm talking about don't bother with flattery or flirtation; they just lay the demand on the line. Abruptly, almost belligerently.

From all accounts, Cinque was of this stripe. I read of one pre-Patty episode when he refused to pay a black prostitute after enjoying her favors, then proceeded to beat her up on the premise that as a vice practitioner she couldn't go to the police for protection. That squares with Patty's testimony of his sadistic pinches, in the breast and pubic areas, when something she said displeased him.

As the swaggering boss of the SLA, Cinque was accustomed to having his way with his harem of white girls. But Patty differs in an important respect from SLA militants like "Mizmoon" Soltysik and Nancy Ling Perry, who out of so-called racial guilt chose to set up house with a thirty-two-year-old escaped convict, ignoring his long record of alcoholism, arrests for robbery, kidnapping and assault, and general instability. In their eyes Cinque, even after cold-bloodedly gunning down Oakland Schools Superintendent Marcus Foster, was a victim-hero, a symbol of racial oppression and a rallying point for revolution.

Patty could never relate on that level. She could feel sorry for someone in trouble—in fact, was rather quick with her sympathies—but they were always directed to a particular individual. I never heard her speak with fervor of an abstract cause. Certainly Patty has no sense of being obligated to make up for the sins against blacks of past white generations, no sacrificial need to make payment by the offer of her body.

The two opposition psychiatrists tried strenuously to insinuate otherwise. Dr. Fort found it "very significant" that the SLA's "code of war" prohibited assault upon or sexual abuse of "war prisoners" like Patty. This was the same self-styled objective scientist who portrayed the 25-inch-deep closet-cell in Daly City as positively cosy, affording "the possibility of both sitting up, lying down, sleeping in a natural position, rolling around."

And Dr. Kozol, in a discussion under cross-examination of Cinque's credibility, proclaimed pompously: "I would take the word of that dead black man." For some reason, nobody challenged this peculiar piece of reverse racism. A known killer, whose brutality and lawlessness were a matter of public record, was allowed to be touted as a more believable witness than Patty Hearst.

Patty and I came close to a direct discussion of Cinque only once. I was telling her of an unpleasant episode at a party the previous evening, where a black government official, a former Corrections colleague of mine, had propositioned me openly in front of his wife. "I don't know where that overbearing arrogance in certain black men comes from," I said. "I suppose there's a history of

70

bitterness behind it. A man who's been through a lot of frustration can be really mean."

Patty looked away, toward the windows of the unoccupied courtroom where we were sitting during a recess break. "I know," she said softly.

That glazed expression came over her face, the one I had learned to identify with the traumas of the closet. For a moment, her pain seemed to hang in the air like a curtain between us. I'm certain in my bones that she was shutting out the recollection of Cinque.

The shocks inflicted on Patty's body—and mind—during those nocturnal visits will not soon be forgotten. Al Johnson used to complain that when he flung an arm around her, she would instantly shrink away. "I don't think she wants *any* man touching her," he ventured.

Certainly it will not be easy, at least for a while, for Patty to enter a close emotional relationship. She'll have to be very sure that any new lover understands the fear that for her now rides with physical intimacy, and that he regards sex as essentially secondary to deeper feelings.

There was one other instance similar to Patty's closet-throwbacks, where events that were separated in time and to me momentarily incomprehensible, suddenly clicked together. That was the Trish Tobin tape: a conversation held between Patty and one of her oldest friends two days after her arrest, and surreptitiously recorded by officials at the San Mateo County Jail in Redwood City. Although spotty and not always audible, and flawed by obvious gaps in continuity, the tape was nonetheless disturbing.

In it, Patty made erratic reference to having acquired a

"revolutionary feminist perspective" that would "create all kinds of problems" for her defense. She also said she was "pissed off" at having been captured by the FBI and did not look forward to a release on bail that would make her "a prisoner in my parents' home."

Trish Tobin, called to the witness stand by Bailey, asserted that Patty had made other, qualifying remarks and that the tape had been edited to Patty's disadvantage by the FBI. The whole conversation, Trish testified, had been choppy, confused, "punctuated with sighs" by Patty: "She seemed rather dazed . . . had no animation . . . didn't seem oriented." In fact their dialogue, conducted by hand-held telephones as they sat separated by a glass partition bisecting the Visitors' Room, was "pretty much a mess." Al Johnson read into the record the FBI's admission that it was "not possible to establish continuity" of the talk.

Yet its effect on the courtroom was undeniable. I myself was puzzled. I could not connect the scattered, rambling rush of words with the Patty I knew.

Except that—somewhere in the back of my mind an earlier alarm was sounding. I had caught a glimpse of just such a disorientation before.

And then I remembered. Weeks back, early in the trial, Patty would be sitting in the car, staring out of the window, and suddenly ask for a pencil and piece of paper. I never asked her what for, but once when she had finished scribbling she explained: "Bailey asked me to write things down whenever they came to mind, because I have such trouble holding on to memories. I'll mention something to him or Al, and then when they ask me about it later, I find it's gone. Things pop into my head—and out again. This way, maybe I won't lose

72

track. I suppose it has something to do with the way I feel about all the things that happened. I want to blot them out, leave them behind. . . ."

She was having the same kind of trouble reconstructing time: "What *is* time, anyway? Sometimes I wake up in the middle of the night, and it's like everything is happening again, right at that moment. No dream—it's happening! Or I'll suddenly flash back ten years—and then draw a blank on where I spent last Christmas. It's like whole segments of time have gotten lost, dropped out of my memory." Her face tightened with distress. "What *is* time, Janey?"

Trish had appeared in court on the morning of March 16. Returning home that night, I went to the stack of press clippings I had been accumulating on the trial. I wanted to refresh myself on certain medical testimony about Patty's mental condition at the time of her arrest.

To begin with, there was the formal diagnosis by Dr. Louis J. West, chairman of the Psychiatry Department at U.C.L.A. Dr. West had been requested by the court, as a neutral authority, to examine Patty at length before the trial. Later he was called upon by Lee Bailey as one of three medical experts put on the stand by the defense. He described Patty's condition as "traumatic neurosis with dissociative features," characterized by "patchy memory disturbance." Professor Martin Orne of the University of Pennsylvania noted that "segments of time" had vanished from Patty's consciousness. And Dr. Robert Jay Lifton of Yale, a specialist on Oriental "brainwashing," saw in Patty's disjointed behavior a classical "survival syndrome" typical of returned POW's who had been subjected to enormous stress. The pieces fitted together.

73

6

As the trial wore on, and my familiarity with Patty increased, an ironic picture began to emerge: elements in her own personality had contributed to the government's claim that she was a willing accomplice of the SLA.

For a starter, there was her curiosity, a genuine thirst for information that recalls her news-conscious antecedents. Patty is interested in everything: ancient cultures, exotic foods (she was appalled that I had no desire to investigate snake dishes), mountain climbing, interior design, aeronautical engineering. When she was locked up in Redwood City, she watched "American Bandstand" on TV whenever she got the chance in order to keep up with the latest dance fads.

She's a good listener—I was struck with her patience in soaking up the most trivial details of my family life—and an avid reader. Her mainstay in jail was an enormous book on Japanese art, but she was also "fascinated" by James Michener's *The Source*, a saga of Jewish history, and kept up with a stream of novels and magazines supplied by her father. Put her in touch with anything, and she wants to know more about it.

This bent of mind would have made it perfectly

natural for her to show interest when Willie Wolfe brought to her closet the prison letters of George Jackson and similar publications, and when Willie reported on the subterranean activity fermenting in the California prison system. These were matters of which she had vaguely read; she would never pass up a chance to hear a first-hand account, especially since it also provided a welcome distraction.

Coupled with her curiosity is a driving perfectionism. Patty cannot tolerate sloppiness, disorder, or any kind of careless performance. Her belt had to be tied properly, not hanging loose. Getting into the car, she would always warn me not to toss her coat casually in the back: "Hang it up, Janey. Fold it properly." As Al Johnson observed in a magazine interview, any room she occupied—even the grubbiest cell—had to be meticulously organized, with her toothbrush and books in their assigned places.

One afternoon, handcuffed, she asked me to get out a cigarette for her. I ripped the package open across the top.

Patty was very upset: "Look what you've done to my pack! Now they're all going to fall out. The right way to do it is like this...." She demonstrated with painstaking care. That was the way everything had to be with Patty: perfect, finished, never halfway. She had the same attitude about learning things. Anything she studied had to be pursued to the end, rounded out to the nth degree.

Once, riding out to the courthouse, the talk turned to weapons. I mentioned to a fellow-deputy that I was using the revolver issued to me. Patty frowned: "In view of my training with firearms—and I did have a lot of training—you should always know your weapon thoroughly, and be sure whether it's going to go off or not. You may fire that thing, and it may not go off at all." She went on and on with a lot of technical detail about firing pins and jamming, with the same kind of academic thoroughness that she would have devoted to a discussion of medieval crossbows.

A similar scene, with black-comedy overtones, took place a few days later, when Patty was scheduled to take the stand to identify the M-1 carbine rifle she had carried in the Hibernia Bank holdup. During recess, she flipped the weapon around a few times and jiggled the bolt lever, scaring the pants off Lee Bailey who had never handled a carbine.

You didn't have to be Perry Mason to see the connection between Patty's thoroughness in gun drill and the elaborate notebooks in her handwriting that were introduced at the trial. The diagrams, corrections, neat little inserts were all typical of Patty: once she got into a game, she did it à la Patty—all the way. Even if she was pretending, playing a role, she had to do it to the hilt: hence the melodramatic, snarling gun-moll performance during the bank robbery.

Behind the perfectionism was Patty's worst burden: fear. I've noticed in prison work that those people who set up rigid standards, who try to program their lives carefully, are usually bent on fending off anxiety. The superorderly arrangement of details is an attempt to put something reassuring between themselves and the chaos of the world outside; it provides at least the illusion of having some control over their destinies.

In Patty's case, the elemental fear is on the physical plane. She's a small girl, delicate-boned, very aware of her fragility in an unpredictable universe. At nineteen, when she was kidnapped, Patty's character had not really taken on definition. Although superficially well traveled and sophisticated, she had been little exposed to the actualities of living.

For instance, until a year ago she was terrified at the mere notion of childbirth. I'll never forget her excitement at the discovery that it was something she could deal with. One night at the Redwood City jail a young girl in a nearby cell was suddenly stricken with labor pains. Nobody else seemed much interested in lending a hand, so Patty stayed and comforted the girl all through the night. "I thought I would be scared," she told me. "At first I couldn't go near her. But afterward I was so proud of myself, I could do it again."

It was her sense of her own inability to cope that made Patty so susceptible to the influence of Al Johnson, an influence that I felt was not always beneficial. In time I came to see that Patty operated in her relationships at three levels. On the surface, especially in public, she was cool, poised, disciplined. At some deep innermost layer, summoned up only in times of severe crisis, she had a core of real strength. But in between, where most of her day-to-day exchanges with other people took place, she was jelly. An underlying feeling of vulnerability made her extremely gullible, maneuverable, ready to turn herself upside down for the sake of getting along with someone she saw as more powerful. It may be significant that her father too has a reputation for being easily swayed, following the advice of the last person he talks to.

Al Johnson had Patty mesmerized. It was amazing to me that a girl so knowledgeable in many respects, so intellectually independent, could be pushed around

77

that way, as if there was a clear split between her reasoning self and a younger emotional self.

Al could dictate the length and color of her fingernails; coax her into scrutinizing a closet that held horrible memories for her; change her mind about liking or disliking a variety of people; forbid her to laugh in front of a camera. Once, when my skirt was ripped and I had to cover it with Patty's coat, that instruction backfired. To Al's great annoyance, she couldn't repress a guffaw. But generally she was his obedient pupil. I felt this handicapped her, stifled her chance of recouping her confidence, growing up and standing on her own feet . . . apart from its dubious effect on the jury.

If a word from Al Johnson was law to Patty, if she would be a good girl just to avoid making waves, how much more compliant would she be in actual danger, under threat of death from a band of acknowledged killers? Patty didn't need their warning about "cyanide bullets"; she was an easy target without that. Slapped during her kidnapping by a rifle butt, she was all too persuaded of their power to hurt. Bottled up in a closet, in constant fear for her life, she was ready to do whatever she had to do in order to stay alive; and, in her genuine terror, to do it with even more than her customary thoroughness, invoking whatever imitative skills she could command. The instinct for survival is a strong motive for the sturdiest among us, including highly trained military men who as war prisoners were put through far less intensive isolation than Patty.

The SLA, whether from shrewdness or by accident, picked their victim well. As a candidate for intimidation, Patty Hearst was perfect.

But by the same token, the idea of Patty as an enthusiastic terrorist is absurd. It collapses completely in the face of two vital, overwhelming aspects of her personality.

Patty has a great craving to be treated as an individual, to be noticed for herself. Even Al Johnson, catching her in a time of great dependency, usually took care to present his instructions within a logical framework. The deadpan facade for the press was to ensure against any accusation that she was taking her plight lightly; the discreet clothes were calculated to wipe out of the jurors' minds the past image of a gun-wielding bank robber.

When Dr. Kozol, the government psychiatrist, addressed Patty patronizingly as "little girl," she bridled; her sense of identity, of personal autonomy, was offended.

But that was precisely what the SLA did, compounded a thousandfold, in trussing her up like a pig and obliterating every vestige of separate, articulate humanity. They made it plain that in their eyes she was nothing more than an object bearing the label "Hearst," a prisoner of war without value except as a tool in their revolutionary struggle. If they had treated her as a *person* rather than an heiress and class enemy, and stressed their humanitarian goals, conceivably—just conceivably—they might have enlisted her respect. But if this was how they went about it—blindfolds, rape, slamming people into closets—no way. She would never want any part of it.

The other thing impossible to reconcile with the SLA is Patty's comic spirit, and the sense of proportion beneath it. Again like her father, Patty is quick to laugh—

even at herself.

Dr. Joel Fort, the unfriendliest of the psychiatrists, had testified that she not only joined the SLA of her own free will but reveled in the international attention that followed. On the day of the trial verdict, Patty and I were riding back to Redwood City at ninety miles an hour under expanded security escort—several State Highway Patrol vehicles as well as extra marshals' cars—when an even larger motorcade came wheeling down the freeway from the opposite direction, sirens screaming and banners flying. Secret Service squads materialized at every entrance ramp. It was the procession for King Carl XVI Gustaf of Sweden, on his first state visit to America.

Patty looked out the window. "Why can't I have an escort like that?" she demanded wryly. "After all, Fort said I was the queen of the SLA!"

Patty has a streak of playfulness, even adventurousness, that pops up often—but never to the point of inviting physical danger. She finds New York exciting—for its theaters and skyline, not for the prospect of being mugged. She could never be drawn into a bank hold-up simply because she was turned on by the "romance" of the idea. That's too loony—okay for *Bonnie and Clyde* or an episode in "Kojak," but not for Patty Hearst.

And when not overcome by panic, she found absolutely ludicrous the self-conscious strutting of the SLA's "General Field Marshal" Cinque, as well as the solemn ceremonials of the organization.

The SLA had an official "theme song," "Way Back Home," adopted from a rock recording group called The Crusaders. Every time it came blaring out of the speaker, according to Patty, they went bananas, acting like a bunch of French patriots responding to the *Marseillaise*.

80

The recording was played in court one day while Patty was on the stand, and she had a hard time keeping a straight face. So did I, sitting behind her. We had just learned that the Crusaders were all Seventh-Day Adventists, who as highly religious people were shocked and embarrassed by the company into which their song had pitched them.

Before resuming the witness chair, Patty had begged me not to laugh out loud: "I can hear you, and I want to laugh with you."

During the recess, she bubbled on: "You know, I just wanted to run out of court and start laughing at that record—but of course, I couldn't. That's the dumbest song. . . . How could they have ever listened to anything like that?

"You know, Janey, when they played that record they were so *serious*. That's the weird thing about it—they were so serious about *everything*. Everything they did meant so much to them.

"Especially that theme song. It was a big emotional thing for them. They would drop whatever they were doing and snap to attention and stare straight ahead like statues. It's like they were listening to the U.S. Marine Band on July 4 playing *The Star-Spangled Banner!*"

There's no place for humor in a revolution—and no place for revolution in the comic spirit.

But the jurors, of course, were operating from different personal backgrounds than mine, and in many ways from a far different point of view.

After 39 days of courtroom sessions, 74 witnesses, 536 pieces of physical or documentary evidence, and a mountainous 1,250,000 words of trial transcript, the case of the *United States* vs. *Patricia Campbell Hearst* went to a jury of her peers on March 19, 1976. Before retiring, the jurors were instructed by Judge Oliver Carter that the fact of a prior kidnapping would not of itself "be sufficient to absolve her of responsibility" for criminal acts committed afterward.

The Hearst jury was made up of seven women and five men. They were a cross-section of middle America: working people and housewives, including civil service employees, mechanics and a dry cleaning clerk. All but one, a stewardess for United Airlines named Marion Abe, were married. Three others had young children or were childless. The remaining eight all had children in their late teens or older, putting them in the position of a parental generation with respect to Patty Hearst. As a group—and I had come to know them well—they were conspicuously intelligent and conscientious.

The jurors reached no verdict that first day. The next morning—Saturday, March 20—picking Patty up at the Redwood City jail, I tried to prepare her for what was certain to be a highly charged and perhaps dangerous moment: "If they decide 'not guilty,' and your parents grab you in excitement and happiness—move close to me, we'll have to get out of court right away. And if it's 'guilty,' and they're sad but still want to hug you—there's a lot of emotion in the courtroom, and your Mom starts crying—don't go over and try to console her. Because then I'll have to get you out in a hurry, and I don't want to make a scene with you."

Patty nodded. "I understand." She was neatly dressed in brown slacks, a white polo shirt, and a colorful knitted blouse.

The wait in the Federal Courthouse that day was agonizing. Patty, Al Johnson and I were in the visitors' room near her holding cell on the twentieth floor. The Hearst family sat in an unused conference chamber near the courtroom, while Lee Bailey paced the corridor outside. Morning went by; time dragged into mid-afternoon.

I had a sense of foreboding. Weeks before, one of the jurors excused from the case because of a death in his family had indicated things were not going well for Patty.

At 3:40 word came that we had a verdict. Patty reacted with a burst of nervous gaiety: "It's all going to be over now, Janey, I'll be out pretty soon!" She was seated directly across from me, with Al Johnson behind her rubbing her back. "Remember the good times we had, the fun dodging in and out of elevators?" She bubbled on and on about how relieved she was, how she looked forward to her freedom—"Now we'll really be able to talk and laugh!" Her words tumbled out a mile a minute, as if somebody had given her an injection of some drug like "speed" and she was unable to stop.

I kept smiling and trying to keep up with her, but deep down I felt melancholy; Patty was so obviously whistling in the dark.

On the way to the elevator, she said, "What kind of drink are we going to have afterwards, to celebrate? I want a tall Margarita."

"Tequila and tonic for me," I said.

"No, make mine a Margarita. Tall."

When we arrived at the courtroom, her father and mother were already in their seats. Mr. Hearst looked trim and outdoorish in a tan sports jacket with elbow patches. His wife was in a dark jumper.

The jurors filed in, led by Colonel Wright. Along with the entire panel, I had developed a great fondness for Bill Wright; his constant good humor had been a big factor in keeping the group on an even keel. A few weeks before, by popular request, I had sat on his lap as part of a celebration for his birthday. He had always struck me as more like a jolly elf than a senior commander in the Air Force.

But he didn't look at all jolly now. And Charlotte Conway, the beauty of the panel, gave no sign of her gorgeous smile.

Colonel Wright handed over a sealed white envelope to the court crier. The judge opened it and glanced at it, and seconds later his clerk was making the formal pronouncement: guilty on two counts, of armed bank robbery and the use of a firearm to commit a felony.

"Oh, my God!" The gasp came from Catherine Hearst, a few feet to my right. Her husband bolted forward in his seat.

Directly in front of me, Patty inclined her head

84

slightly and murmured something to Lee Bailey. Then she turned back and stared straight ahead, her face suddenly a frozen mask. But I had some idea of what was churning inside.

I was stunned myself, shaky, dimly aware of a trembling in my limbs. All I could think was, "I've got to get her out of here, away from people."

Lee Bailey was consoling her. I came up quietly and took over, slipping an arm around her waist and guiding her toward the door. We were both tense but dry-eyed, each hanging on to her feelings for her own reasons. Patty was not going to become a pitiable public spectacle; I had an obligation to the dignity of the Marshals Service.

But when we reached the privacy of her holding cell, our façades collapsed. Both of us broke into tears. We clung to each other, sobbing out our sorrow. "I knew what was coming," Patty whispered. "But I couldn't face it. Who was I fooling? They made up their minds about me two years ago—from the night I was kidnapped in Berkeley. That's what I was asking Lee in the courtroom: did I ever have a chance?"

An image from the bullring flashed into my mind. I don't like bullfights, because the bull never really has a chance. He may score a few points along the way—fight back, even gore the matador—but in the end he has to be dragged out, lifeless. He is doomed from the moment he enters the ring—in fact, earlier—from the moment he is chosen (or kidnapped?) from his herd to be the victim-star of the correo.

Now came a realization that had up to then been thrust aside: I was no longer a disinterested observer of Patty's fortunes. Somewhere in our sharing of strains

85

and excitements, of romantic confidences and laughter, an attachment had grown up between us. Her moods, her problems mattered to me. In spite of every resolution, I had become involved.

My reaction to the verdict, incidentally, kicked up a stir, mainly because of some sloppy reporting. Two or three correspondents, either eager to dress up their stories or carried away by the drama of the moment, wrote that I had broken down publicly in the courtroom, abandoning my custodial role. This produced a flurry of letters supporting my right to "express an emotion"—and also some flak around the Marshals Service, to the point where I felt obliged to make a statement straightening out the record.

For the moment, my concern was with Patty. After the blow of the verdict, she had an absolute dread of facing the press photographers. And they, of course, were bent on getting a picture on this climactic day. If we took our normal elevator route down to the basement, two cameramen from the regular "pool" would be waiting, inescapably.

I appealed to Phil Krell, Jr., the deputy marshal in charge of media arrangements: "Everybody is trying to get at her, Phil. It would be cruel to let them, today. Can't we get out some other way?"

Phil agreed to look into it. He led us out into the hallway, then disappeared for a moment to see what he could figure out. Nervous—there were people I didn't know, all over the place—I poked my head around the corner of the corridor.

Patty grabbed me and pulled me back: "Don't you stick your head out! You're just as noticeable as I am. And wherever they see your face, they know my face

86

isn't far away!"

Phil came back. He had worked out a route using the fire escape, and we got down to our car on Polk Street without being seen. However, a crowd of photographers half a block away spotted us clambering in, and sprinted in hot pursuit. "Duck!" I told Patty; as she crouched in her seat, I covered her with my arms.

Pulling up at the jail in Redwood City, we were spotted by waiting newsmen again, even though we used the rear entrance held in reserve for emergencies. Seeing the cameras poised for action, I simply let go of Patty and told her to run as hard as she could. She took off like a streak, down the stairway, and nobody was able to get a picture.

Later, my supervisor grumbled about it: "You know, she could have gone running in the opposite direction." But I never had any worry about Patty pulling that kind of surprise, and in fact she never did.

What I remember most about that afternoon was Patty's amazing courage. She would be facing, when she returned to court for sentencing in three weeks, a possible maximum term of thirty-five years. Yet on the ride back to Redwood City, she was calmer than I was. She had little more to say about the verdict: "People who are celebrating now over my conviction will be singing a different tune in a few years, when the whole truth comes out." And, "I know two people who are really happy now. Can you guess who?"

No, I couldn't.

"Bill and Emily Harris"—the surviving SLA kidnappers.

Whether bank robber or victim, I thought to myself, Patty Hearst has to be rated a person of tremendous strength. If—as I did not believe—she in truth was guilty, if she actually did embrace the murderous SLA, then her toughness in hanging onto a false position and refusing to be shaken from her claim of innocence was staggering.

If on the other hand she was a victim of naked terrorism, who survived only to be put through the second agony of a kind of legal crucifixion, then her courage under the burden of double martyrdom was almost beyond comprehension. She had once remarked that it took a crisis to bring out the reserves of a person's strength: "You never know how tough you are until you have to be."

I thought back to her heritage: daughter of the board chairman of the powerful Hearst Corporation; granddaughter of the stubborn eccentric who founded the newspaper dynasty; great-granddaughter of Senator George Hearst, who determinedly built the Homestake lode into what became the largest gold mine in America. The Hearsts had a history of single-minded resolve.

My own Mexican-American background was more volatile. That evening, there was a gathering at the home of one of the deputies. Many of the people who had been assigned to the trial were there. The atmosphere was exuberant; "the government" had won an important victory. The more I heard the expressions of satisfaction buzzing around me, the more miserable I became.

Suddenly an older woman, the wife of one of the deputies, bounced across the room. "Come with me, Janey," she said.

She led me into the bathroom. "Now, you just cry, Janey. Let it go." I did, bawling my head off for several minutes.

Behind my tears was the sorrow over Patty, and also at parting with the jury. Over the weeks of our confinement together, they had become my good friends. And although we had complained to each other of our weariness during the last days of the trial, and had looked forward eagerly to our day of "liberation," now that it was here we had a sense of loss. Something familiar was going out of our lives.

Many nights, I had sat up till dawn while they slept behind doors that were wired to record the slightest movement. And every morning I greeted them in court by our agreed "high sign": an index finger rubbed across the bridge of the nose. I respected their earnestness: once, as we were dining out, the canned restaurant music was interrupted for a news summary—forbidden to their ears; they promptly launched into a loud "Happy Birthday" to drown out the broadcast. And at times I joined in the familial fun. My newlywed friend, Linda Magnani, was accustomed to signalling a greeting at 7:15 A.M. every day to her husband on the street outside, by drawing the drapes in her room twice. Late one night I offered the jurors a suggestion. The next morning when Dan Magnani came by, *all* the jurors drew their drapes simultaneously.

About a half-hour after the verdict, the jurors had sent word that they would like to say goodbye to me before being taken to their homes. As it happened, I had just left Patty in the holding-cell area for a brief conference with her attorneys. So, still in a semidaze, I slipped down to the basement.

The jurors were piling into a bus. Looking at them, I felt mixed emotions: glad that they were at last going home, sorry to be losing them, sad about Patty. . . .

Then Linda saw me, and threw her arms around me, and for the next few minutes it was just a mass of arms and tears and kisses, everybody hugging and sniffling at once. I started to cry, and somebody said, "It's all right, Janey, you go ahead," and then I realized they were crying, too. One of the men said, "We understand, Janey. You're sad. Well, we're sad, too."

I thought he meant, sad to be saying goodbye. I now realize he was giving me my first clue to a most remarkable phenomenon: the post-verdict anguish of the Patty Hearst jury. I asked for the foreman, Colonel Wright—and learned that he had fallen ill within minutes after delivering the verdict. He had requested and received private transportation to his home—but not before stumbling into the men's room and throwing up. I thought to myself, "He's a good man, a kind man. He couldn't *stomach* what they were all doing to Patty."

Some weeks later, at a jurors' reunion party, I was approached by Helen Westin, a gentle, comfortable middle-aged housewife from suburban Mill Valley. "Oh, Janey, Janey!"

"What's the matter, Helen? What's wrong?"

"I can't explain it, Janey, but—ever since I made my decision, I haven't felt right."

From Helen's story, some mysterious ailment had descended on her since the trial, a nervous condition similar to shingles. She was supposed to be leaving the next day on a month's vacation with her husband, but she didn't think she was going to make it (she was right).

Over the next several months—in fact, for a full year—I would hear more and more of the jurors' doubts and misgivings, of their outright regrets, and of the repercussions of the trial in their personal lives. I was able to piece together the sequence of their deliberations, and the factors that most influenced their decision . . . a decision which, I am quite reliably informed, they would not be likely to repeat today.

On retiring to their 35-foot jury room, a special chamber normally reserved for judicial conferences, the panel had promptly and without argument selected Colonel Wright as foreman. He was their senior member, well liked, and had served on courts-martial.

The colonel led off the discussion, querying whether the government had actually established a beyond-reasonable-doubt case. As he proceeded with his summary, along lines distinctly favorable to Patty, there were some frowns among his listeners and some exchange of questioning glances. But nobody interrupted.

He stopped, and for several seconds there was a heavy silence. Nobody seemed eager to question their leader. Finally Marion Abe, the airline stewardess, spoke up. Marion is a tall, self-assured brunette of Japanese-American background, one of the few jurors who never lowered their guard with me. She had stayed apart from the other women on the panel but spent a lot of time playing gin rummy with the men.

She was not satisfied, Marion said; there were a number of points that had no clear explanation.

Bruce Braunstein agreed—and everybody came to attention. Bruce was the house intellectual, a slight, bearded man who shaped and sold pottery from his home in Napa. He stayed in his room a lot, playing the flute; when he talked, it was deliberately and well.

Bruce had a feeling that something was being held back from them; that what they had witnessed when Patty was on the stand was a carefully rehearsed performance, controlled by her lawyers: "We don't really know what she's like, whether we were looking at a live girl or a robot." Didn't any of the others get that impression?

It turned out that, thus encouraged, they did. Patty had come across to them as remote, baffling. Now and then someone had caught a glimpse of what seemed to be a more genuine personality, a flicker of reality, only to have it disappear into the shadows a moment later. The effect was tantalizing, frustrating. Were the defense attorneys staging a show, playing games with the jury?

Older members sensed there was something more to the mystery, that Patty herself was pulling back. Either way, the almost-visible screen surrounding her made it hard to evaluate the rest of the case.

Without a clear view of the defendant, they were confronted mainly with reams of psychiatric theorizing, and the "hard" evidence of documents and tapes. Instinctively they opted for what seemed most tangible, what they had seen with their own eyes or heard with their ears.

Photos had a powerful negative impact, especially the shot of Patty riding to court with her manacled hands clenched in the Black Power salute. A close second was the picture taken by the cameras at the Hibernia Bank, showing Patty positioned in battle regalia between Cinque and Nancy Ling Perry. Why, the skeptics demanded, if she was being kept under close guard by the SLA, would they so place her that her captors would have to risk hitting each other if they shot at her?

Of the many tapes carrying Patty's voice, the one hardest for the jurors to dismiss was her jailhouse conversation with Trish Tobin, presumably spontaneous in its toughness and apparent rambling defiance. To that, the female members of the panel in particular added the "little stone face," the Mexican figurine found under Willie Wolfe's body whose twin was among the contents of Patty's purse when she was arrested. The women jurors could not believe that a girl who had for a time been intimate with a man—under whatever circumstances—would still be holding onto a gift from him sixteen months after his death unless there had been a genuine attachment.

And many of the panel could not accept the blanket explanation of "mind control" offered by UCLA's Dr. West. Why couldn't Patty give herself up during the long period when she was a fugitive? Why did she choose to stay within visiting distance of Bill and Emily Harris, if she feared and hated them?

After the break for lunch, Colonel Wright called for a ballot. The vote was ten to two for conviction. The dissenters were two of the youngest jurors, newlywed Linda Magnani and Philip F. Crabbe, II. Phil is an Oakland postman: serious, bespectacled, father of three small children. A former student at Berkeley, he speaks softly, throwing in an occasional quiet chuckle.

With the sides clearly defined, the debate grew more heated. Oscar "Doug" McGregor leaped in. Doug works for the Army Corps of Engineers, and is the father of seven children. Deceptively casual in dress and manner, he pounced on the "mind control" defense. What exactly did Dr. West mean by the phrase "coercive persuasion"? He didn't understand it, and he doubted that anybody else did.

Linda Magnani flared up. "Would it make any difference to your vote if you did understand it?"

"No, it wouldn't."

"Then look it up in the dictionary when you get out!"

Some of the older women held back, troubled. Marilyn Wentz prided herself on being a liberated woman, in sympathetic contact with her three daughters ranging in age from fifteen to eighteen. Another juror had a son of twenty-odd years, living with his girlfriend. The arrangement had been a wrench to her morality, but she had learned to accept it.

Bruce Braunstein, too, was conscious of conflict. He had reservations about the effectiveness of the entire penal system as an instrument for rehabilitation.

Everywhere there was a growing sense of discomfort, of unhappiness or at least reluctance in facing the duty ahead. But when a second ballot was taken, the vote was 11 to 1 for guilty. Linda's resistance had crumbled. That left Phil Crabbe—silent, soft-spoken Phil—as the only holdout.

The afternoon had worn away. At 5:00 P.M., Colonel Wright called a recess "to let everybody sleep on it."

But Linda Magnani couldn't sleep—not a wink. As she later told me, all through the night she had tossed in her bed at the Holiday Inn, wondering if it had been right to change her vote, wishing she had a chance to talk the problem over with her husband, an investment counselor. Could she really take it upon herself to send Patty Hearst to prison? She hoped that somehow she could fight her way through to a clear answer.

When she arrived at the courthouse at 8:45 on Saturday morning, light-headed and bleary-eyed, she still had not been able to. A new ballot was taken. The tally still was 11 to 1.

Marion Abe, who had been first to speak up on behalf

of the prosecution, turned her persuasive talents full-blast onto Phil Crabbe. She couldn't shake him. Helen Westin tried; then Cleo Royall, a pleasant shop employee with a sixteen-year-old daughter; finally, two of the men. Still no dice.

Marilyn Wentz gathered together a stack of documents, left her seat and pulled up a chair alongside of Phil. A buxom, attractive dental assistant with thick curly hair, she put an arm around her fellow-juror and asked him to go through the material with her.

The others sat quietly, watching and waiting, as she picked up a photograph, examined it, and passed it without comment to Phil. Item by item they went methodically through the file together. No one spoke.

At long last Phil Crabbe looked up, a strained expression on his face.

Was he ready for another ballot, Colonel Wright asked?

Phil sighed. "Yes."

And so, after twelve hours of deliberation, the Patty Hearst jury found the defendant guilty.

A small unnoticed irony attended the vote. Of all the jurors who had been sitting on the case, the one most quickly and firmly committed to Patty's side was Mary Nieman, an alternate who sat at the extreme right side of the box. Small, intent, her gray hair in a Buster Brown cut, Mary was very much a loner; she caused me many an extra night's duty by insisting on remaining by herself while the other jurors were out dining together.

But her sympathies had been evident for some time. Viewing the closet at Golden Gate Avenue, she alone among the panel had recoiled in horror. And after the verdict she told reporters that she would have held out for acquittal to the end, causing a hung jury. Whether or not anyone else responded to her arguments, "I don't think they could have convinced me."

But, although one of the other original alternates was called in to serve in the course of the trial, Mary was not. So Patty lost her most staunch defender.

However, for most of those who did vote, the end was only the beginning. They quickly discovered that it was all but impossible to discuss the subtleties of the case with their families or friends; people who had not been through their dilemma simply could not understand it. The jurors could relate comfortably only to each other. Instinctively many turned to their bearded guru, Bruce Braunstein, for clarification and consolation; his phone was ringing constantly.

Several of the women felt that they might find mutual support in regular reunions. The first one was held in May, two months after the verdict, and I was invited. All the jurors except Marion Abe and Mary Nieman came. One after another they posed the anxious question to me: "Did we do the right thing, Janey? You know her better than anybody. Tell us."

All I could answer was that yes, they had made a fair and honest judgment according to the material that was available to them; but that I felt Patty was the victim of circumstances, circumstances of which they were not completely aware.

Couldn't I say more than that, something that would put their minds at rest?

"Look—you were a fine jury. If I were going on trial, I'd be happy to put my fate in your hands. I hope that from my book you'll be able to see the rest of the

Patty breaks the "no-smile" rule that prompted jurors to query whether she was "a live girl or a robot." Janey perceived a "three-level personality": cool surface, strong core, but in between "pathetically vulnerable."

Juror Mary Nieman, Patty's firmest supporter on jury, emerges shaken from visit to SLA apartment hideout. An alternate, she was never called. At right, with glasses, is Colonel William Wright, foreman, who became ill after delivering verdict.

Paul Sakuma

Paul Sakuma

Linda Magnani, the youngest juror and a newlywed. She joined Phil Crabbe in voting for acquittal on first ballot. Sleepless before final tally, she "wished she could consult her husband."

Paul Sakuma

Bruce Braunstein, "bearded guru" of the jury. During the trial, Braunstein was put off by Patty's apparent icy calm. Later he came to see the whole case differently.

Hearst jurors, haunted by "doubts and misgivings," find solace in frequent reunions. Here, with Janey a year after verdict: Bottom row, from left: Charlotte Conway, Richard Ellis, Bruce Braunstein, Helen Westin. Middle row: Beatrice Bowman, Robert Anderson, Stephen Riffel, Marilyn Wentz, Oscar McGregor, Philip Crabbe.

Girl graduate: June, 1974. Janey's open-minded views as a minority member — "as long as we share the planet, we ought to get along together" — created problems for her at San Diego State.

Janey in uniform as Correctional Officer, with her mother, 1975. She had joined the Metropolitan Correction Center in San Diego in order to aid hard-pressed, poorly educated *chicano* prisoners.

Janey's late father, Raymond, with, from left Janey, Pam, Stella, Yvonne holding Martha, father holding John. "I wish I could get my father back for one minute. . . . He would have been so proud."

Still "queen of the family," Janey's 88-year-old grandmother, Maria Estrada, is flanked by Janey and her mother, Frances Jimenez. Mrs. Estrada hitchhiked 1,000 miles to U.S. border to escape Pancho Villa's bandits.

The deputy departs. Janey turns in her gear on resigning from Marshals Service, July 30, 1976.

Patty's father, Randolph Hearst, squires Patty and sister Anne at Anne's coming-out party in 1973. With him, said Patty, "the only thing you could be sure was that you'd have a marvelous time."

Patty with ex-fiancé Stephen Weed. She took a dim view of his book—and of him. According to Patty, Weed told the SLA kidnappers to take anything—"so they took me!"

Fiery finish of the SLA: Los Angeles, May 17, 1974. Patty "sat mesmerized" watchi
bloody shoot-out on TV as announcers reported she was probably inside.
Uncompromising police action convinced her she was a social outcast.

William (Willie) Wolfe: Was
SLA soldier Cujo actually
Patty's "tutor-sweetheart," as
government claimed, or an
"irresponsible sloganeering
rapist"? Janey heard no
hints from Patty of emotional
involvement; "only a kind of
detached disgust."

Wide World Photos

Steven Soliah, Patty's boyfriend
during her final fugitive days. When
he was acquitted in fatal robbery
despite her testimony, Patty
wondered aloud: "Would I be
crying or happy if they had
convicted him?"

United Press International Photo

Patty, after collapsed lung, in hospital cell at Metropolitan Correction Center, San Diego: "like anybody's kid sister . . . except for the drained, empty eyes." Patty often reminded Janey of a doomed bull in the *correo*.

Happiness, Unlimited: Ex-deputy and her new friend get together at Hearst's Nob Hill apartment to celebrate Patty's release on bail. Whatever happens, Janey will "never be far in spirit from her corner."

story—what kind of person Patty Hearst is."

An informal gathering brought six jurors together in September, and the panel held another reunion three months later. With time they became more haunted, not less. There were many post-mortem discussions in search of greater understanding of what had happened. Several felt that Lee Bailey had let them down, as well as his client; that he had started off with a bang, gotten embroiled in a private duel with prosecutor Browning, and faded away in a feeble summation. There was general agreement that Lee had wasted far too much time and energy in trying to discredit Joel Fort. Certainly Fort's smugness, his sweeping pronouncements were obnoxious; but Lee wouldn't let him get off the stand. Bailey kept nagging, fussing, worrying away at incidents that occurred nearly twenty years ago, to the point where the jurors grew bored, then resentful.

In addition, Bailey and Al Johnson were faulted for putting Patty on the stand at all. Here the jurors were curiously in tandem with an authority they had chosen not to believe, Dr. West, who had insisted that Patty might be legally qualified to stand trial, but that she was nonetheless not "psychiatrically competent," that is, not in appropriate emotional condition.

Criticism was voiced also of Judge Oliver Carter, first for permitting the Hearst family—but not the general public—to attend the jury selection. The silent presence of the Hearsts, it was felt, dominated the courtroom. Prospective jurors directed their answers to the judge, but kept their eyes on Patty's famous parents. Nobody felt free to admit a prejudice against the Hearsts, or bias in their favor.

Again there was the feeling that by instructing them

to weigh Patty's "whole course of conduct," the judge was "putting her on trial for everything," leaving the jurors at sea about where their attention should be focused.

The speculation about their own responsibility continued, and continues. At a first-anniversary-of-the-verdict meeting, to which I was invited, several would report drastic trial-related changes in their personal lives. With the exception of Marion Abe and Mary Nieman, who have dropped out of the group, all had by 1977 arrived at a new viewpoint which would be articulated for me by Bruce Braunstein.

I had my own theory about their conviction of Patty. To me, there were subtle influences in the background, subliminal factors, that nobody fully acknowledged.

The publicity build-up before Patty's capture by the FBI had been tremendous. As Linda Magnani said during jury selection, speaking of the bank robbery photos, she wasn't sure she could "block those out."

Secondly, many Americans have an unspoken hostility—right or wrong—toward entrenched wealth. They don't like to see the rich "get away with anything." Joel Fort's reference to Patty as "a queen" in the SLA army was a not-so-subtle jab at exploiting this latent prejudice by associating her with her grandfather's "Lord of San Simeon" image.

The whole character of the defense, which relied not on a simple, human presentation of Patty as she truly is but on highly technical psychiatric testimony, went against the grain of the jurors. To counter the bulky physical evidence of the prosecution, Bailey and Johnson offered only an abstract theory that was simply too insubstantial for the jurors to accept, perhaps even to grasp. They were impatient, for example, with the detailed analysis of Patty's speech patterns by Dr. Margaret Singer—relevant, to my mind, as it was; one juror grumbled that such dry theorizing seemed to belong either to the nineteenth century or to some futuristic age of science fiction—but not to the era of live television with its gut-level accent on immediacy and action.

"He's talking over our heads" was a frequent recess comment about Dr. West—which raises another question. Is a conventional "jury of peers" the best possible body for evaluating a situation loaded with psychological and medical complexities? Is such a procedure fair to either defendant or jury? I was to hear more about this, in eloquent terms, from a seasoned psychiatrist in Salisbury, Rhodesia.

Foremost of the hidden pressures, in my view, was Patty's role as a symbol of youthful revolt: what you might call the generational overtones of the case.

Patty was tried in an atmosphere still tense with the kids-versus-parents battles of the late 1960s—the crashing disillusionment on one side, the rising bafflement and anger on the other. After the clashes over Vietnam, drugs, beards, the pill and women's lib, many parents felt rejected, neglected, betrayed. New values challenged their conduct of national affairs and of their lives. Whatever the virtues of individual jurors, they had to bring some of that collective bitterness with them into the courtroom. I think it's no accident that two-thirds of the jury that convicted Patty were of her parents' generation, and that the last two to yield were among the youngest on the panel, members of Patty's "peer group" who could identify with her.

In this setting, the prosecution's evoking of a "generation of rebels" had to produce some effect; likewise Joel Fort's allusion to Patty as an experimenter with marijuana, LSD, and mescaline, even though marijuana is now being widely decriminalized as less dangerous than alcohol. It's hard to go through an American college today without taking a passing fling at "grass"; but that's a long way from bank robbery.

Crucial in this respect was the Trish Tobin tape, which I feel was heard and judged by the jury not so much for its content—scattered, at best—as for its slangy, irreverent tone.

My generation—and Patty's—has its own vocabulary, worlds apart from that of our mothers and fathers. "Uptight," "where it's at" and "very together" don't translate easily into earlier terms. We use four-letter words freely, as a badge of the new openness and sexual equality. Our "fuck you!," however shocking to our elders, is an absolute commonplace that may even be an expression of affection.

Curiously enough, Patty's mother, for all of her Catholic conservatism, understood this point and mentioned it to me after the verdict. But for most of the jurors, Patty and Trish might as well have been talking Albanian. Patty's phrase "a prisoner in my parents' home," must have raised a lot of hackles, reinforcing the displeasure over her failure to call her parents while she was a fugitive.

The jurors never heard Patty's out-of-court explanations of her long silence. "I was afraid to call them," she told me on one occasion, "not only because I felt rejected, an outcast, but because of something I heard over the radio. Charlie Bates (the FBI chief in San Francisco)

100

was quoted as saying that if I turned myself in, 'we'll give your daughter all the help she needs.' To me, that meant he thought I was crazy. Maybe my parents did, too—so they'd have me put away."

On another key issue, the celebrated "little stone face" given to Patty by Willie Wolfe, the jurors were again hampered in their evaluation by their lack of contact with the real Patty. They could see only a souvenir from an ex-lover—kept for many months, hence meaningful.

But for Patty, an art history major with a fanatical interest in ancient cultures, the figurine had a different kind of meaning. What nobody on the defense side bothered to point out—and Patty's lawyers don't seem even to have realized—is that Olmec sculpture is, as I remember from my Mexican culture studies, among the unique and preeminent art forms of the world.

The Olmecs of Mexico were the oldest known civilization in America, probably direct ancestors of the Mayas of Yucatán. Besides carving massive stone heads of eighteen tons and more, they created smaller stones in jadeite and basalt, described in the *New York Times Encyclopedic Almanac* as "delicately incised . . . unrivaled for balance, form and beauty." The subjects were old-time pagan deities.

This was what Patty, rightly or wrongly, thought she had. Museums and collectors prize such "monkey-faces." Anybody with even a casual interest in art history would welcome one. A real buff like Patty would automatically treasure it. Not to guard it among her private possessions would be unthinkable.

As if all this were not enough, there was the haunting business of Patty's emotional inaccessibility. A robot doesn't win friends and influence jurors. As Bruce Braunstein put it to me soon after the verdict, "Maybe someday you'll be able to tell us whether she was really herself on that stand, or a different person ... what she's really like. Maybe when we know that, we'll be able to draw other conclusions as to whether we made the right decision or not."

I knew what he was talking about. All too often I had seen Patty "disappear": at Stanford Hospital, under the stress of our visit to the Golden Gate Avenue apartment, sometimes even without visible outside stimulus, prompted by some passing thought. The common clue seemed to be the SLA rapes. Thumbing back through the trial testimony, I wondered whether Patty's memories were simply too shattering for her to face. Said Dr. West, "Each time I would come back to certain moments like the night of her kidnapping or what had happened to her when she was put in the closet, there would be the same kind of collapse ... her voice was almost inaudible." When Dr. Martin Orne asked about the closet, "She would look at me and say 'Do I have to talk about it?' " Months later, Dr. Robert Jay Lifton of Yale found her "still locked in that trauma and deeply confused ... terrified when required to talk about the details of her ordeal."

Even the antagonistic Dr. Harry Kozol testified that when pressed for comment on Willie Wolfe, Patty "became very much upset, began to shake and quiver, obviously suffering."

All through the trial, then, Patty's mind was flashing on and off protectively, more intent on preserving the balance toward which she was struggling than on winning the case. First things first: survival rather than

102

risking the return to the pit of pain and confusion.

Why had this fact eluded the jury? For one thing, it had not been particularly emphasized in the defense summation. In spite of all the muttering about high-priced and showy lawyers giving wealthy clients an unfair advantage, things don't always work out that way. Furthermore the jurors, unlike myself, had no contact with a natural, hair-down Patty against which her emotional departures could be measured. The girl they saw was largely a fiction, a mixture of hearsay and design.

Patty first came into public view as a restless schoolgirl, all but buried under the shadow of her famous name. Then, the portrait of a Patty still only half-formed fell into the hands of a series of people for whom she was to various degrees an exploitable object: the SLA, intent on creating a caricature that would serve their propaganda purposes; the FBI, seeking to recoup their declining prestige by staging a spectacular woman hunt—first for kidnap victim, then for "common criminal"; and lastly the media with their swarms of feature writers, TV interviewers, and photographers.

Piled onto all this were the well-intentioned efforts of her attorneys. Anxious to cancel out the militant image first circulated by the SLA, they counseled a tight-lipped reserve. Since this reinforced Patty's own impulse toward headlong withdrawal, they succeeded only in fashioning a grave unsmiling robot, and replacing one caricature with another.

To the jurors, grappling with diametrically opposed psychiatric theories of Patty's behavior, her mask of detachment was the final insult. The reticence urged by her lawyers, the flights from reality urged by self-preservation could only be interpreted as an attempt at concealment. What was she hiding? Not innocence, presumably. . . .

Both sides were trapped: the jury, by their obligation to render a decision on the basis of available evidence; Patty, by external advice welded to internal needs. Here were the components of classical drama, in which a hero or heroine has no possible exit, but marches to inexorable doom . . . as Patty did from the moment she was snatched up by the SLA. After that, any move she made had to compound her troubles.

I would suggest that the Patty Hearst case, which has provided a Roman holiday for so many onlookers, is actually more like a Greek tragedy; that Patty has been the consummate victim—of social upheaval, generational tensions, and old-fashioned legal tactics—victim above all of wounds inflicted on her mind and body by her SLA captors, whose threats of vengeance still haunt her. For minimal survival she has had to take refuge in a withdrawal that gave the appearance of shiftiness, Nixonian "stonewalling" . . . and hence of guilt.

Meanwhile, the jury's decision met with general public approval. People interviewed for newspaper and TV polls were not kindly disposed toward Patty. Usually, Americans respond to the underdog. But Patty didn't fit any of our popular images. She wasn't a cheery working girl like Doris Day or Mary Tyler Moore; not a bereaved widow (Jackie Kennedy Onassis) or loyally suffering wife (Pat Nixon); nor was she a sunny hoyden with a heart of gold (Shirley MacLaine). The leftists denounced her as a traitorous publicity hound; the squares said she should be disowned by her parents. She even inherited some of the anger felt over the pardoning of Richard Nixon. No matter that one was presidential schemer, the other kidnap victim; why should there be a special standard of justice for the powerful? Let Patty Hearst be punished—and condemned.

And yet when people had an opportunity to see Patty up close, behaving naturally, their hostile opinion was quickly reversed, as I discovered a few days later on a trip with her to Los Angeles.

8

In the week that followed her conviction, Patty had a new set of visitors at the Redwood City jail: interrogation teams from the FBI. During the trial, she had been instructed by her attorneys not to answer any questions about her activities in California after returning from hideouts in the East in the fall of 1974. So she repeatedly took the Fifth Amendment when asked about various crimes attributed to the radical underground in the Bay area, pleading fear of reprisals against herself and her family.

Now, however, Bailey and Johnson were concerned not only with winning a lenient sentence in the San Francisco case, but with the potentially more troublesome charges Patty faced in Los Angeles. On May 16, 1974, she had fired twenty-seven submachine gun slugs into a sporting goods store there to cover the escapes of her SLA companions, Bill and Emily Harris, after Bill had been detected shoplifting. Patty had never been able to explain her behavior as other than a kind of fear-conditioned reflex, a response to continuous SLA drilling. Furthermore, in her flight with the Harrises afterward, she had taken part in a series of car thefts and two brief kidnappings.

Bailey and Johnson reasoned that at this point full cooperation with the government might improve their client's prospects on all fronts. So suddenly their order was reversed, and Patty started talking. According to later disclosures by the FBI, she began filling them in on numerous bombings and other actions, as well as the identities of latter-day SLA sympathizers and ideological feuds in the underground.

Her dialogue with the FBI was interrupted by an order from Los Angeles requiring Patty's presence for arraignment in Superior Court there on Monday, March 29.

We were assigned a special Coast Guard plane, a big four-engined C-130, for the trip down to Southern California and back. For Patty, who had seen nothing but cells, courtrooms, and crowded highways for weeks, the occasion was an outing. She looked forward to soaring through the clouds, high above her troubles.

A team of deputies drove us out to the airport. In accordance with FAA regulations, I removed her handcuffs before we boarded the plane. With my supervisor, we hurried up the boarding stairs, snack lunches stashed in my briefcase. At the top platform I paused to blow farewell kisses to my colleagues; to my surprise, Patty did the same. She was in unusual good humor.

"Presidential special," she quipped as we entered the passenger section; there were rows of empty seats to choose from. The two of us settled in over the wings. She seemed delighted to have her hands free, and after take-off even the security-conscious Glen Robinson didn't seem to mind. At ten-thousand feet, where could she go?

The plane carried a five-man crew, a youngish clean-cut bunch who might have been college jocks a few years back. From the fish-eye glances directed at Patty, it was clear that this twenty-two-year-old convicted bank robber was not their candidate for Queen of the May.

However, one of the mechanics, Mike Stubbs, plumped himself down across the aisle. He had a nice manner and a friendly grin. Soon he and I were chatting away. Mike wore the silver insignia of the air crew: eagle's wings stamped "A.C.," with the Coast Guard shield in the middle.

Wings—like rings—are among my strongest weaknesses. I asked if I could have them.

"Sure." He started unpinning the clip.

Patty, at the window seat, leaned forward to catch his eye. "Me too! Anything Janey gets, I get half."

"Uh-uh." I shook my head. "I'm the boss. That gives me unusual privileges."

"That isn't fair," Patty protested.

"Oh yes, it is."

After a few minutes, I asked if I could go up front to the cockpit. Mike nodded.

Again Patty didn't like being left out. I said I would check with the crew up front to see if it would be all right to bring her.

It wasn't. To a man, the response was negative: from Jerry Myers, the pilot; his copilot; radioman-navigator Carl Elsner; and Joe Mauro, the flight engineer.

"Come on, fellows," I told them. "Don't make a judgment till you've given her a chance. She's really nice. You have to get to know her, then see if you can still say you don't like her."

"Well—okay. Just for a minute."

Patty came running in, brimming over with childlike

excitement. Personally, I was content just to enjoy the view, but she couldn't rest until she had satisfied her curiosity: found out which was the "stick" and which the throttle, how the automatic pilot could correct the plane's position with the flick of a knob, when the altimeter reading was important. She asked every question in the book, and picked up fast on the answers.

Her enthusiasm was irresistible: "What a fantastic gadget," as she studied the "bubble," in which a tiny replica of the plane floated in liquid to duplicate its movement. Could she try on the parachute jackets strapped along the wall? And listen to the radioman's earphones? He must be getting mysterious messages in code. . . .

Carl Elsner took off the earset and solemnly handed it over. Patty was startled to hear a blast of rock music.

Everybody laughed with her. By this time the "just-for-a-minute" restriction on her visit had been forgotten.

Was there any chance, Patty wanted to know, that we would get to see San Simeon from the air?

"We fly right over it."

Soon the vast Hearst estate was spread out below us, the largest privately owned acreage on the Pacific Coast. Directly ahead loomed the castle complex, a marble and alabaster fairyland gleaming in the early morning sunshine.

"There it is, Janey—there it is! Isn't it beautiful?" Patty was jumping up and down, pointing over the pilot's shoulder. The plane dipped obligingly, to what looked like a couple of thousand feet. "See that guest house on the right? I used to stay there when I was small, with my uncle Bill [William Randolph Hearst, Jr.] and aunt Bootsie. My Dad would come up in his private plane, and we could see him flying over. I'd run out waiting for him to land, and I always used to wonder what the castle looked like from up there. Now I know!"

"Wow, that's really a castle," one of the fellows said. "Must have sixty or seventy rooms."

"Exactly one hundred," Patty told him. "Thirty-eight bedrooms, thirty-one baths. The first-floor vestibule is paved with Pompeiian mosaic from the year 60 B.C. The assembly room is 84 feet long by 35 feet wide."

And this girl, I thought to myself, has been cooped up without bitching in a windowless nine-foot cell!

Patty rattled on happily with her tourist-guide spiel: all about the white marble Roman pool with its quarter-million-gallon capacity and the stately colonnades leading to a Neptune Temple; the private chapel, furnished with the treasures of a half-dozen European monasteries; the guest houses, which were really Italianate palaces. She just couldn't shut up—eyes sparkling, cheeks aglow—and the effect was really lovable. I could see the astonishment—and appreciation—breaking out on the faces of the crewmen, the expressions that said, "This kid is really a gas!" As we zoomed southward, and the buildings of the castle receded into miniatures, she was giving the fellows an inside account of her grandfather's animal cemetery.

We stayed up front for practically the whole flight. When the radioman started talking with Los Angeles airport, we knew it was time to go back to our seats. Patty took a last look around, as if trying to memorize the gadgetry. One of the crewmen—I think it was the copilot—came up to her. "I hear you've been looking for wings."

110

"Yes, I have."

"Try these." He took off his insignia and handed them to Patty. I don't think she would have been happier with a Nobel Prize.

After we landed, the entire crew came down to see us off. The pilot handed me his card: "Give this to her. And tell her that any time you need us, we'll be more than glad to be at your service."

Each of the others, in his own way, communicated the same message: "You were right about Patty. People would have to like her—if they only had a chance to know her."

Despite the polls supporting Patty's conviction, thousands of people felt that way about her anyway. Sympathy and affection for her were running themes in the letters that had been pouring across my desk since the beginning of the trial. As a result of the worldwide exposure given the case, and my constant presence in the photos with Patty, I was a magnet for all kinds of individuals who were deeply stirred by the unfolding controversy.

Letters started flowing in right after my first contact with Patty, while I was still at Marshals School in Georgia. They came from Iran, Guam, Toronto, St. Thomas, and Rhodesia, as well as European capitals and every corner of the United States. Nine-tenths were friendly; if I had accepted all the invitations to visit, I could have lived as a houseguest for years. The writers ranged in age from sixteen to nearly eighty, and in occupation from artist to truck farmer. Many were doctors; some were behind prison bars.

A high proportion of the mail was of a religious nature, from well-wishers of every creed. Some listed the special prayers being recited on Patty's behalf; others sent rosaries, crucifixes, and in one case a crocheted Easter egg for forwarding to her. A Hungarian refugee in Canada showered me with devotional leaflets. And a solemn letter postmarked San Jose, California, declared that "the road to salvation is through me." It was signed "Jesus Christ."

Another major, but far different, category was mash notes. I don't flatter myself that I'm all that devastating. But the hinterland has a lot of lonely people floating around, living on fantasies dished up by movies, television, and magazines. They're looking for a likely target to fix on. I suspect any presentable face will do, especially if it's attached to an event being played up by the media.

The romantic pitches varied from the bluntly sexual, which I never read beyond the initial foaming-at-the-mouth obscenities, to the whimsical and quaint. A forty-year-old engineer in Minnesota observed that he "wouldn't mind being in your custody . . . permanently." From Oakland, "You seem like a very intellectual person"—so how about lunch? A man in Greencastle, Pennsylvania, ventured that after reading his credentials, "You might call me up and consent to marriage."

Among other volunteers were a twenty-three-year-old musician "impressed with your maturity, strength and devotion to your job"; a newspaperman in New Haven in search of a "really beautiful" pen pal; a TWA pilot from Paramus, New Jersey; and a poetry-writing janitor who urged me not to worry about my unmarried state. There was also a sprinkling of advice from elderly gen-

112

tlemen, including a retired farmer in West Virginia who had "two boy friends for you; one plays horn in a band."

I heard from occasional critics, like the fellow-deputy in Texas who objected to my concern for Patty: "I too would like to be human, but there are other things more important" (he didn't say what); and more often from admirers who praised it. A sixteen-year-old girl in Verbank, New York, and a policeman in Florida wrote that I had inspired them to seek careers in the Marshals Service.

A gratifying theme, sounded in many letters, expressed relief that I had been on hand to cushion Patty's ordeal. Virginia Reuterskiold, a retired woman doctor from Rolling Prairie, Indiana, told me I had every right to be upset by the jury's guilty verdict: "To me that means you were showing compassion—a quality to be nurtured wherever found. You probably were with Miss Hearst many times when she needed just such an understanding. I don't mean my statements to indicate my personal reaction to Miss Hearst's case because that is irrelevant to your position which concerns me just now.

"Whenever an item about Miss Hearst appeared on television I looked for you—not only because you are a lovely-looking person and a pleasure to see, but also because I was always impressed with the capable and efficient manner you had with Miss Hearst—ushering her—as it were into and out of rooms and cars and through crowds with quiet dignity. In fact I had the feeling that you were making a special effort to keep yourself in the background. . . .

"I hope you have by now reconciled yourself to whatever criticism you have unjustly received and know in your heart that however you reacted was *right* for you.

Those who don't understand that are the ones who have reacted wrongly—not you."

Her view was echoed by a computer executive in Chicago, who felt that my "very obvious humanitarian attitude" might not have won friends for me in the Justice Department but had nonetheless earned his respect. An Associated Press reporter sent me a private note attributing to envious government colleagues the story that I had lost emotional control: it wasn't the first time, he declared, that someone had been jealous of a minority-group employee rising too far and too fast— and it wouldn't be the last.

On the bizarre and unpredictable side, I had letters from a self-professed lady bank robber eager to surrender, but only to me; from the mother of Steven Weed, accompanied by a favorable review of his book, apparently in the hope that I would try to soften Patty's disapproval; and from a men's shop in Carteret, New Jersey, that wanted an autographed photo to display in their window. For opposite extremes there were letters from a Georgia sharecropper enclosing three pennies for Patty (with apologies; he had nothing more), and from a modeling agency in New York offering me a lucrative contract (this was followed up by a call from their local representative, who refused to believe I had set my sights on a more active, less artificial career).

The letters that impressed me most were those from psychiatrists and mental health specialists, particularly a long and thoughtful handwritten communication from Dr. Nelson Daniel of Salisbury, Rhodesia:

"Dear Miss Janey Jimenez: I feel desperately sorry for this girl Patty, though news is hard to come by here. Noted one point that touched me deeply, in *Time*

114

magazine, the paragraph where her two sisters cried as did US deputy marshal Janey. I feel there is someone around to help her.

"It's my medical training and age—60—hence, experience—that cause my worry. To be beaten by one's enemies and then crushed by one's friends leads battered minds like Patty's to crime and sometimes suicide. So if you can watch over her, and give her the love and the tenderness that is in your heart, this must be a great help. . . .

"In my honest opinion, Christ would have said 'Sister, go in peace, sin no more.' Can you raise any clerical friends to petition for her?"

In a postscript, Dr. Daniel asks if I think that "Patty's wealth went against her?"

And he adds a comment on the possible limitations of trial by jury, very much along the lines of my own reflections:

"The march of time demands change; the medical world is a good example. However one aspect of law, 'Trial by Jury,' would appear to need further thinking, as the best way to justice given certain circumstances. Where the fate of a person rests upon technical points, points beyond the comprehension of the jury, and more especially where the prosecution and defense expert witnesses are in complete disagreement, then surely a jury cannot be expected to render a verdict in due fairness to the accused.

"In this respect, the trial of Patricia Hearst is worthy of further consideration. The basic point at issue would seem to have been her 'state of mind.' On this point the expert psychiatrists voiced opinions that varied in the extreme, points quite beyond the ability of the jury to

115

understand. Now, I am medically trained, and had I been on that jury my answer must have been, 'I just don't know'; hence, 'Not guilty.'

"In the mid-eighteenth century William Blackstone said, 'Better ten guilty persons escape, than one innocent suffer.'

"It would seem that the jury, being ignorant of this girl's 'state of mind' and heeding the Blackstone words above, were bound to give a verdict 'Not guilty.' I suggest that Patty was very unlucky, and that the jury exceeded their duties, possibly influenced to some degree by the press."

Seven thousand miles away from Dr. Daniel's office in Africa, a woman Ph.D. candidate in psychology wrote to me from Duke University in Durham, North Carolina. Jean Anne Matter began by congratulating me for "doing even more than Angie Dickinson to improve the image of female law officers," then asked me to pass along a letter to Patty that was enclosed. If that proved not feasible, "I hope the good vibes will reach her anyway. Seems she'll need all she can get to come through this with her sanity intact."

In her message to Patty she expressed the wish that she could somehow "mail you strength and wisdom to get through this god-awful mess. . . . Whenever I see your determinedly composed face whisk across my TV screen, I think, 'There but for the grace of God and the fact that my father ain't rich, go I.'

"This in turn leads me to become exceedingly irritated when I hear these fruit-nibbling morons suggest that because you lived with your fiancé and perhaps harbored a few (gasp!) liberal ideas, you were on your way to perdition even before your life was suddenly and violently snatched from your control. What a crock of toenails!

"You sound like a common, garden-variety, well-educated, and reasonably well-off woman under thirty. Since I also classify myself in those terms, my indignation when I hear you (presumably) slandered is partly selfish, I suppose. But it also annoys me that people assume, when something bad happens to somebody, that somebody must have deserved it. In psychological jargon, this is sometimes called the 'Just World' phenomenon. People sometimes have difficulty acknowledging that evil things really can happen to innocent people since this requires the acknowledgment that evil things can happen to one's self, even though one has done nothing to deserve misfortune."

The letter went on to note that among professionals engaged in the study of personality, interpersonal understanding, and human motivation, Patty was "rapidly becoming a classic problem in the field," frequently cited in academic theses. "The question is, under what conditions will people attribute your actions to something about you (personal disposition); and under what conditions will they attribute your behavior to something external (situation or pressure)."

Ms. Matter concluded with the wish that she could "make everybody go away and leave you alone," so that Patty would have a chance to "take hold of your life again, decide who and what you want to be and who you want to be around. It's going to be a while before you can do that . . . finally coast out of chaos and are again able to exert active control over your own destiny."

Such letters, from sensitive and obviously informed observers, reinforced my conviction that I was not mis-

117

judging Patty's case. But what spoke directly to my heart was the surprising volume of mail from prison inmates—like the Mexican-American in Michigan's Kent County jail who was "very proud" of me, and the youth in Stringtown, Oklahoma, who was making me the subject of an oil painting.

Without exception these correspondents were sympathetic to Patty—"rotten deal" was the recurring phrase—and warmly approving of the way I had treated her. Several mourned the absence of such moral support in their own lives, saying it might have made a decisive difference.

Of course, there was the usual quota of fanciful sentiment—sexual deprivation is one of the unpleasant realities of being locked up—but even these had an engaging flavor: "I know it's not very kool [sic] writing to someone as beautiful as you and talking about something that's impossible ever to have ... but I want you to know there's a lot of dudes that think you're super-bad and would like to get in touch with you including me." The writer was very concerned about Patty: "I pity her for getting mixed up with a bunch of jive turkeys, and everybody is down on her but never me."

From the Cummins Prison Farm in Grady, Arkansas, came an elegantly handprinted letter with a single line in Arabic script across the top, followed by the Islamic date of Sha'ban 5, 1396. After a gracious "Salaam," the author noted that this was "really the very first time" he had ever "communicated with a law enforcement officer willingly," then launched into an earnest request for my views on current "moral, intellectual and spiritual life."

In the prison correspondence as well as among the

general population, my Hispanic name was clearly a factor. A twenty-four-year-old named Ralph Martinez, serving time in a Midwest institution, sent me a photo of himself with his parents. He hoped I would not be put off by his convict status, "but I couldn't lie to someone that looks as nice as you do. . . . It would be nice to know someone out there cares something about me."

9

On April 12, Patty was back in Federal Court for sentencing. Judge Carter decided that before making a final ruling, he would like to see the results of another psychiatric study. So he ordered her committed to the Metropolitan Corrections Center in San Diego for several months for that purpose, technically under maximum sentence of thirty-five years. On the way to San Diego she would make another court appearance in Los Angeles in order to have a trial date set there.

She had not up to then yielded an inch in morale. Her triumph with the Coast Guard crew two weeks earlier had demonstrated that despite the bruising hours of SLA terror, endless flight from the FBI, seven months of stifling incarceration and nerve-pounding trial, her spirit remained intact.

It was her body that crumbled.

Our follow-up trip to Los Angeles, this time by helicopter, was scheduled for Wednesday morning, the fourteenth. For me, it would be the end of a grueling siege in which for ten weeks I had had little rest and virtually no time for myself. I was looking forward to an Easter holiday with my family in Van Nuys, the luxury of uninterrupted sleep, and then a round of visits among old friends in San Diego. For the moment, at least, Patty Hearst and I would go our separate ways. Our period of intimacy, I thought, was over.

Actually, it had just begun.

I spent most of the evening of April 13 in San Mateo shopping, trying to catch up with a huge backlog of gifts unsent, wardrobe neglected. It was 9:00 P.M. before I got home to my apartment in Daly City.

I heard the phone ringing from the hall, over and over, insistently. Someone was very determined to get me.

It was Glen Robinson, my supervisor. His voice was sharp with irritation: "Where the hell have you been?"

"Out shopping. I've got to go right to bed now, Glen, so I can get up at three. Patty and I have to be out at the airport at six."

"You're not going anywhere tomorrow."

"What do you mean?" Something in his tone alarmed me.

"Patty is sick. Very sick."

My heart froze, plunged down a bottomless chasm. Until that moment, I didn't realize how close Patty and I had become.

She had been rushed to Sequoia Hospital in Redwood City, Glen said, by the San Mateo County sheriff's office, after the doctor at the jail had pronounced her case a medical emergency. "She's having problems breathing."

"Is it a heart attack?"

"I don't know."

"She's only twenty-two!"

"They think maybe it's a collapsed lung. She's been in surgery."

I had seen prisoners with collapsed lungs in institu-

121

tion hospitals. Painful. And scary.

"Who's with her, Glen?"

"Barney and Erna." That was Barney Harrington, one of the older deputies, and his wife.

"I want to go there."

"There's nothing you can do."

"I can *be* with her."

"Tomorrow."

"No—right now."

"You stay home, Janey. That's what I'm going to do. I'll take you out there tomorrow."

"Please, Glen. I'll be at your office in twenty minutes."

It was a quarter to eleven when we arrived at the hospital. Patty was doped up but conscious, a tiny figure lost in the big white bed, her thin pale face framed against the pillow by masses of chestnut hair.

I walked in. The instant Patty saw me, she began sobbing. "Thank God!" she whispered. "If I can't have my family here, there's nobody else I would want to have."

It was an eerie moment for me, terribly moving and not quite believable. This girl, who had been brought up with everything, actually needed me. . . .

I felt myself going mushy inside. Up to this point I'd been able at least to avoid displaying emotion publicly; now I knew it was more than my controls could handle.

"What happened?" I blubbered. "Is this your idea of an Easter present? I know—you just don't want me ever to get home, you old stinker! What are you going to pull next? We just can't get rid of you!"

I rattled on, afraid to stop. It was one of those times when you joke to avoid falling apart completely. As the

122

poet Byron said, "If I laugh, 'tis that I may not weep."

"Okay," I said, "I know you didn't want to go to L.A. because you'd have to run into the Harrises in court, and you'd do practically anything to avoid that. But you didn't have to go to *this* extreme!"

Patty had referred often to her fear and loathing of the Harrises. She thought they had very possibly been behind the bombing at San Simeon during the trial, and she was convinced they would stop at nothing; that any time either of them was near, her life was in danger.

My far-out joke about her two tormentors drew a faint smile from Patty. "You're right. This has to be the hard way out."

I bent over the bed and put my arms around her. "How did it happen?"

She had just finished a lengthy afternoon of interrogation by the FBI, Patty said, and was walking back to her cell, when she was hit by a sudden, uncontrollable attack of coughing. Afterward, she couldn't breathe. Panic swept over her. "I knew that sooner or later, something would happen to me physically. With all that smoking, and not enough sleep, and the food that I couldn't eat . . . plus the pressure of the trial, and then the FBI interviews. I just never expected trouble with my breathing."

There had been other strains, she now admitted, since the verdict. For one thing, she had been upset by my press statement denying that I had broken down in court. She felt the news stories about a law enforcement officer being so touched on her behalf were helpful to her general case; why, she wanted to know, had I repudiated them?

"Because they weren't accurate, Patty. And I have a job to keep."

She nodded contritely. "I'm sorry, Janey. I'm really making your life difficult."

She had been concerned also about what living conditions she might face in the Metropolitan Correction Center at San Diego, where she would be undergoing her "ninety-day-study." Up to then she had only been in a jail, for temporary detention; this would be a full-fledged prison. Was the food better than at Redwood City? Could she use her crocheting needles and her nail polish? Were the girls allowed to watch TV? Above all, were the personnel—I had once been on the staff—friendly?

Those anxieties, I felt, were part of the reason she had ended up in this hospital bed.

Patty didn't want me to leave; but I could see that her nurse took a different view. "Go to sleep now," I told her. "Get a good night's rest—that's what you need most."

"Will you be back in the morning?"

"I don't see what else I can do. I can hardly take that helicopter down to Los Angeles all by myself. Now, you be good. I don't want to hear about any more stunts while my back is turned." I hugged her again and went out.

In the corridor, Glen Robinson took my arm. "Let's go get some coffee."

We found a small cafe still open a few doors down from the hospital. Glen led me to a table in the back and, after we had ordered, faced me very soberly: "I've got to tell you this, Janey. You've become too close to Patty. Partly it's our responsibility; we let it happen, by the situation we put you in. We're sorry about that. But now it's got to stop. You're altogether too involved."

This wasn't the first lecture I had had on the subject. The day after the verdict, Chief Deputy Brophy had warned me against displays of emotion. "I realize this is an unusual case," he said. "Hopefully, we won't have a Patty Hearst case again. But you'll have to remember in future, whoever the prisoner is, to keep your distance."

According to Glen, I was wide open for trouble, riding for a bad fall. Patty, he declared, was a girl from another class: cold, selfish, with no real feelings for anyone else. "Janey, after she's released and gone, she's going to forget about you. She'll say 'Ah, so she helped me for a while—big deal.' I'm afraid you're going to get hurt, Janey—really hurt—and you're too kind a person to be subjected to that."

I was very aware of Glen's sensitivity and his concern. But I felt he was wrong about Patty: "I just don't think she's that kind of person."

"You've got to realize," he went on, "she comes from a different, opposite world to yours, out of a different background. She doesn't look at life the same way. Tell me this, Janey: suppose it was ten years from now, or five, and she was out, in the clear. . . . Suppose she's walking down the street, maybe with some friends, and she comes across you lying in a gutter, dying. . . . Tell me, would she have the time to help you, to give you a dime, a nickel, a cup of coffee?"

At that grim picture, I burst out bawling, like a little kid. Glen pressed his point relentlessly. "No, she wouldn't, Janey. You know that. She would walk away."

There was nothing much I could say even if I'd been able to talk, which I wasn't. I was too busy using every napkin in that coffee shop to soak up my tears. Finally I managed a few words. "I—I realize she'll have a lot to do when—when she gets out," I stammered. "Friends to call, people to see. But someday—I'm sure that someday I'll hear from her."

"Be serious, Janey. For heaven's sake, be realistic."

I went to bed that night feeling very empty.

The conversation with Glen haunted me for the next two days. I could never accept generalizations about race or religion or social class; to me they were clichés that robbed people of all individuality and reduced them to identical ciphers. The conventional grumblings among some Mexican-Americans about *anglos*—that they "stole this country from us, we were here first," or that they were "basically nasty, not to be trusted"—have never held much water for me. I think I can trace my attitude back to my grandmother, who when she arrived at the American border sixty-odd years ago as a penniless teenager was treated kindly by a total stranger, an *anglo* lady rancher. My grandmother spoke often and feelingly of the pot of dinner leftovers, the converted chicken house that provided shelter against the fierce night wind, and the made-up carpentering job that enabled their party of five refugees to earn a few cents. She would brook no catch-all complaints about *anglos*; people were people.

Nor have I in turn ever been able to get worked up about labels. I know Mexican-Americans who scream if you call them *chicanos*, and others who won't answer to anything else. Personally, I'm Janey Jimenez. If that translates into *"chicana"* for some people, that's up to them; they can call me whatever they like. To those who ask my nationality, I say "American," since I was born and raised here. If they persist about "background," I say "Mexican," without any fancy percentages about Spanish or Indian or French.

My attitude created problems for me at San Diego State, where Mexican-Americans had their own society—MECHA—supposedly dedicated to promoting the culture and welfare of our minority. I joined; it sounded to me like a fine goal. Then I found out that *anglo* students—no matter how friendly, how well-informed, what they had to contribute—were barred.

That sounded silly to me. I couldn't follow MECHA's reasoning. As far as I was concerned, we were all on this earth together. We all go to the same place when we die; as long as we share the planet, we ought to get along together, regardless of race. I dropped out.

That didn't go over very big with my fellow-*mexicanos*. Strolling to class, I would be taunted as "white-eyes lover." They thought the only color I could see was white. And I thought color didn't mean a damn; it was how people treated each other that counted.

I knew that Patty felt the same way, in common with most of our generation. During her engagement to Steven Weed, she had worked for a time at Capwell's Department Store in San Francisco. When the clerk force there, largely from minority groups, launched a campaign for higher wages, Patty pitched in enthusiastically. She made no distinction between *anglos* and anyone else: people who did their jobs well deserved a decent salary. Period.

After that unsettling conversation with Glen, I couldn't keep sitting on my tension for very long. Tears came up every time I thought about Glen's forecast, but I had to find out how Patty felt. Alone with her as she was finishing breakfast, I blurted out, "Glen says you'll

127

never call me."

Patty looked startled, but didn't make any answer. I guess I took that for confirmation. I raced on, the sentences tumbling out one on top of another: "I think I've been kind enough to you, Patty. I don't think everything's been done by the book. I've made sure not to mistreat you the way everybody else has—trying to get your autograph, hoping maybe you'll do a favor for me—which I know you can't do but I wouldn't have tried to exploit anyway. I've had nothing in my mind except just being nice to you. You treat me humanly, so why can't I treat you humanly? You do everything I tell you to do, so why should I expect anything from you but kindness?

"Glen says it's a mistake for me to go on thinking that way; that once you're out of this situation, I'll never hear from you again. He says if you saw me lying in the gutter, you wouldn't give me the time of day."

Patty eyed me very levelly. She seemed to be putting her thoughts together. "That," she said finally, "is what's wrong with people. They keep on judging me because of where I was and who I was with for the last two years. Why don't they ask me what I would do?"

She didn't add, and I didn't ask for, anything more.

I was reminded of her words three and a half months later, when I left the Marshals Service on July 30. At eight the next morning—the opening day of my return to civilian life—I had a phone call from Patty at the Metropolitan Correction Center in San Diego. Previously she had been forbidden to communicate with me as a deputy marshal. Now she was seizing her first opportunity to call me directly as a friend. She did not lose an instant to underline the point.

128

Patty's first few days after the lung collapse were extremely trying—and not only because of her discomfort from the surgical tube implanted in her chest. She had been transferred to a room in the maternity ward, because it was isolated and easier to secure. But her presence was no secret; and the hospital staff, like the people at Stanford Hospital, descended on their new celebrity like vultures. They found excuses for running in and out of the room to look at her. When Patty murmured something about coffee, a stream of attendants fell all over each other to bring cream—milk—sugar— and take a peek. You couldn't have had more service at the Mark Hopkins. Except that Patty's personal possessions—pencils, hair ribbon, a memo scribbled to her mother—were vanishing into the pockets of souvenir hunters.

The morning after she was brought in, there was a squabble over security arrangements. Al Johnson wanted them left in the hands of the county sheriff's office—which was simply impossible under government regulations. Federal prisoners are the responsibility of the U.S. marshal.

Al huffed and blustered at me, complaining that federal deputies were "less familiar with the area." I brought in Glen Robinson for a face-to-face confrontation, whereupon Al backed away. It was "just a matter of geography," he muttered. After Glen left, Al rebuked me for "making an issue" of his interference.

As ever, Al was a mixed blessing. I had grave doubts about the value of his presence. He had a tendency to talk down to Patty; I didn't think he really understood her. On the other hand, Patty appreciated his promptness in rallying to her bedside: "Bailey phoned, but Al *came*, the way I would with a friend."

In spite of making this distinction, she was quick to defend Bailey against any criticism. She never had a bad word for his trial tactics. And when one of her visitors, the wife of her cousin Willie Hearst, complained that Lee had made personal capital of the case with his lectures in Las Vegas and frequent press interviews, Patty retorted: "But he was working on his arguments all the time. You just don't know." And to me she made a point of insisting that it was not lack of concern that kept Bailey from the hospital: "He cares, all right; he'd be here if he thought I needed him. But he knows my parents and Al come all the time."

The fourth night of her stay, Al spent some time visiting with her, then called us from outside to say Patty was at the pit of despair: "She gets that way once in a while, when she feels totally alone, abandoned . . . and she won't trust even me."

I went into the room. Patty was staring at the ceiling listlessly. "Nobody cares," she told me. "My big mistake was to carry out orders so carefully for those twenty months while I was out there. Maybe I should have fucked things up some way so that now I would be dead!" She turned her head away.

After a while I went out and peeked around the corridor.

"Get back in there!" Glen ordered. "I don't want her left alone. I don't trust what she might do to herself." He suspected that the lung collapse was a kind of involuntary attempt at suicide, a reaction by the body to a diminishing will-to-live. If it had indeed been brought about by depression, he said, the next time she might be provoked to a more active attempt on her own life.

130

Certainly she was showing the classical symptoms for potential suicide laid down in our Corrections Officers' training course: physical illness, sleeplessness, a sense of isolation, withdrawal. . . .

I went back to Patty's room and started scouting around, checking tables and drawers.

"What are you doing?"

"Just looking to make sure there's nothing you can kill yourself with." I figured that with Patty, a blunt thrust was the way to flush her out.

"Where'd you get that idea?"

"From Glen."

She managed a weak laugh. "Forget it, Janey. That's one thing I wouldn't do—now, or ever."

It turned out that an incident that occurred during the trial had left a strong impression on Patty. Her cell at Redwood City was located next to the "tank" where drunks, pickpockets, drug addicts, and other overnight inmates were kept. Late one night a girl was brought in, disheveled and distressed. For the next few hours Patty heard the stranger intermittently ripping and scraping away at her skin, apparently with a safety pin or needle.

At dawn she saw the girl again, covered with scratches, unsightly, bleeding.

Patty shook her head emphatically. "That's not for me, Janey. No way!" Relating the incident seemed to bring her out of her funk.

So the crisis over "suicide" passed. But there were others ahead, including one with her parents that strained to the utmost the bonds between Patty and myself.

The Hearsts were on Patty's doorstep from the very
first day after her surgery: father, mother, and a stream of
sisters. They came to the hospital bearing candy, flowers, magazines—and love. It was really touching to see
their concern.

Mostly it was expressed in a form dear to Patty's
heart—or at least her stomach. Patty was a gourmet who
had been confined to jail rations. As long as she was a
federal prisoner, she could not have food brought in
from outside. But now, in her ambiguous status as
prisoner-patient, gift packages were permissible: even a
glass of wine, on the medical grounds that it might
stimulate her appetite.

Her parents started by apparently buying out a Jewish
delicatessen. Patty sat up for a feast of bagels, lox, cream
cheese, and herring. The next day, they shifted to crab
and ice cream. When I came in that evening, Patty told
me the crab was still being held in reserve: "Ask the
nurse; it's in the refrigerator." At Patty's coaxing, I
agreed to "test it." It was the best crab I've ever tasted. I
kept nibbling away, until Patty fixed me with a quizzical
eye: "Well, Deputy, would you say it's okay—all right to
eat?"

Every time her parents came to visit, as they left they would take her room-service order for the next day: "We'll be back tomorrow, Patty. What can we bring you?"

Mr. Hearst in particular was sweet, approachable. Since Patty was on the same floor as the maternity ward, visitors used to pass a lot of babies on the way to her room. Once, running into him in the corridor, I remarked that the infant squalls and incubators were kind of getting under my skin: "It all makes me feel as if I'd like to have a baby. How about you, Mr. Hearst? Would you like to be a grandfather? Or would it make you feel old?"

"Not at all. I'd love it. But that doesn't mean I ever will. Gina feels the world is overpopulated . . . and none of the other girls is even pointed in the direction of marriage." He seemed genuinely disappointed.

"Your turn will come."

"I hope so, Janey. I hope so." Then he brightened up. "The doctor says Patty is coming along very well. I've brought a book that I think she'll enjoy." And he hurried off.

I looked after him, marveling at his devotion, frankly envious. Here was a girl who for a year and a half never made a phone call or sent a post card to her parents—and they welcomed her back as if she hadn't been away ten minutes. I thought to myself, they must really love her. *I* wouldn't have been greeted that way—not with a roast or a turkey, but with a smack on the behind. . . .

I was particularly impressionable on the point because I was going through a painfully contrasting experience of my own. I had expected to be back in Van Nuys on April 18, the Sunday after Patty's illness, for

133

Easter dinner with my mother, brother, and sisters. I hadn't seen them for some time, and occasional letters and phone calls weren't enough. I missed them.

Like Patty, I was part of a five-sister household; in my case, fourth in line rather than the middle girl. I was closest to the sister directly following me—Stella—just as Patty is to her sister Anne. But my mother, of course, was at the center of the family, so when it became obvious by Good Friday that I wasn't going to be able to get away from the hospital for the weekend, my mother was the one I called. I explained the emergency that had come up, expecting that she would share my disappointment.

She hardly seemed aware of it. "That's all right," she said calmly. "It's just another holiday."

"But Mom—I feel terrible! I promised you and the girls—"

"It's okay. You have your job to do, they need you, you stay there. Your work is important."

"But I wanted to be with my family." I was crying by now.

"Just be careful to eat properly—and sleep well."

Sleep well! I hadn't had a decent night's sleep in weeks. Was that all I meant to my family—a name in the paper?

I groped once more for some expression of caring. Was she sure she didn't mind?

"Well, I have five more children. One child less at the table isn't going to make any difference."

That was the crusher. It opened up some old wounds. As far back as I could remember, there had never been any affection—or even sympathy—from my mother. Not once during the years when I was growing up at home

134

did she ever tell me she loved me. When I was a little girl and ran into a problem at school, it was always the teacher who was right. I was seventeen before I was allowed to have a date, and eighteen when I got my last spanking. Only after I had moved away, two years later, did my mother say anything about loving me—and then not in person, but in a letter.

Like Catherine Hearst, she was terribly concerned with the proprieties, with how things looked to other people. At our home, the carpet was always laid out for visiting children; but for her own kids, forget it. Except for my brother.

My decision to pursue college and a career was received glumly; good Mexican-American girls got married young (as all my sisters have) and stayed home. When I phoned from agents' training school in Georgia on Thanksgiving Day of 1975, lonesome and homesick because all the East Coast trainees had gone back to their families for the holiday, my mother told me: "Well, it was your own choice to be a deputy marshal. You'll just have to stick it out."

I went to her for guidance once, after Patty's trial, when Al Johnson asked if I might be interested at some future point in serving as one of Patty's private bodyguards. It didn't sound very appealing to me.

"Do it," my mother advised. "The girl needs you. God will repay you someday." My mother is an ardent Seventh-Day Adventist. She confided that all through the trial she had been watching Patty on TV, praying for her constantly.

Praying—and weeping, as she was beginning to do now.

I was too angry to speak. That reaction, I felt, was

typical of her: tears for an utter stranger, but none for her own daughter.

No doubt there were reasons. Her own path had not been the smoothest. Her mother—my grandmother, still queen of our household—had traveled on foot and in railroad box cars nearly one thousand dusty miles from Zacatecas, northwest of San Luis Potosí in central Mexico, to impoverished safety across the United States border, a seventeen-year-old refugee from Pancho Villa's rampaging bandits. One of her brothers had been murdered before her eyes.

My mother had been married young, and saddled before she knew it with six children and a charming husband who loved us all dearly but could not accept the responsibility of a family. As a construction worker, he drifted in and out of jobs, sometimes unemployed for months. He walked out on us all when I was four.

The trouble was, he never made the clean break which might have allowed my mother to start a new life. He paid her support money and he came around now and then to kiss and fondle us. I'm sure my mother never stopped loving him—he was a handsome man, a good person at heart. She hasn't even gone to dinner with anyone since his death—but his visits always ended in quarrels.

Everybody suffered. My mother developed an extreme bitterness, warning her girls that no man was to be trusted. That advice plagued my adolescence and has shadowed my emotional relationships since; I'm always testing instead of trusting.

Nor was the situation any better for my father. He craved the affection of his daughters, but didn't know

136

how to earn it. And we were torn between our instinctive need for him, and loyalty to our mother. One evening when I was about nine, he took my mother, my eldest sister, Yvonne, and myself for a ride. Yvonne was very abrupt with him. After she and my mother went inside, I lingered behind a moment.

"Janey," he asked softly, "do you hate me too, the way your sister Yvonne does?"

I didn't answer. I didn't know how to answer.

"Don't you love me?" he went on.

I couldn't look at him. "I—I guess not." And I ran inside.

That conversation still haunts me. I wish that somehow I could get my father to come back for one minute from wherever he is, so I could tell him how I really feel, how I've always felt. . . .

My father made one last stab at reuniting the family. In 1966, he went to one of my aunts and told her he had resolved to take up his duties as husband and father, whatever the cost. Later that night—it must have been close to 1:00 A.M.—he came to the house and knocked on the door.

My mother refused to let him in; everybody was asleep.

"I want to see the children," he called out. "I have something I must tell them—all of them!"

"Come back at a decent hour."

A pause. Then his footsteps trailed away.

The next morning he was hit by a car. A week later, his message still undelivered, he was dead.

One of the great frustrations of my life is that my father never lived to know how much he meant to me, never saw me finish college and enter the Marshals Service.

He would have been so proud, and he knew so few rewarding moments.

The first few days at Sequoia Hospital Patty was still having her low moods. She was weak, not entirely out of the woods physically, and there had been an accumulation of stresses.

When her sister Gina came, Patty barely spoke. Afterward, Gina came up to me in the hall: "What's wrong with Patty? Bob and I used to be so close to her, and now we just can't get through. Is it because she's been incarcerated, locked away from us? Or does she think we're mad at her?"

"No, she knows by now that you're not mad at her."

"Of course, we were all separated for a while. As young girls we went our different ways . . . me to England, Cathy to L.A., Vicki up north; but ever since the kidnapping we've closed ranks and hung together. It's made us understand each other better, realize what we've missed, how much we need one another. But Patty, being the catalyst, has been outside that. Which is ironic, since she's the one that brought us together."

"Plus," I agreed, "she can never be really alone with you. There's always someone from outside the family in the room—me, or some matron. That has to make everybody a bit self-conscious."

"Well, I can tell you, I'm not happy about it."

I tried to reassure her. "Just be patient. Someday she'll be able to relate, but right now, with no privacy and somebody down her throat or sitting on top of her every minute, it's hard. For all of you."

Good Friday, two days before Easter, was a bad day in the hospital room. Patty's morale was shaky, and mine

138

was worse. Not only was I still smarting from the cancelled visit home—and my mother's indifference about it—but I had just been informed that I would have to work through the entire weekend. There simply weren't enough female personnel. I was weary, fed up, and not at all cheered by the prospect of having to get out of bed an hour earlier Saturday morning to pick up another deputy on the way to the hospital.

To compound my frustration, I couldn't even reach my colleague on the telephone to complete the necessary arrangements. Patty saw me brushing away a tear.

"Now you're all bummed out;" she said. "What's the matter?"

"Oh, not a thing. I merely have to make a pick-up at dawn tomorrow—which means practically zero sleep tonight—work through the whole Easter weekend—"

"I thought you were getting somebody's wife to fill in for you one day."

"No. She's got kids. It would be ridiculous. I'm the logical candidate."

We were both silent a moment, staring at the whitewashed walls. Finally Patty spoke. "If it wasn't for me," she said slowly, "you'd probably be home right now. Enjoying your family and your vacation."

"Oh, that's no way to look at it, Patty. You didn't do anything; you were *done* to. And then things just piled up for everybody."

Again we lapsed into silence and long faces. It was Patty who put a stop to it. "Hey," she said, "we haven't got room for *two* bummed-out people around here—and I'm the one with the tube stuck in my chest! So, Deputy—stay out of my act!"

I had to laugh, and from then on things eased up. Patty

139

drifted off early into a relaxed sleep.

But when I came in Saturday morning, she was glummer than ever. Her surgeon, Dr. Weissberg, had been around early and warned her that unless she wore special nylons in bed, she might develop blood clots in her legs. To Patty, in her dejected state, that meant there was a strong possibility she would never walk normally again. First, according to her gloomy accounting, she had taken a terrible psychological pounding; now she felt her body was "falling apart." Her lungs had gone first, her legs would be next. She was no longer, she concluded, a healthy young girl.

I pointed out that the special nylons were a routine precaution, not a sign of doom. She was making good progress medically with the aid of a respirator machine, and there was really no reason to worry.

She didn't seem to hear a word. Apparently the doctor had gone further. From Patty's account, he had sketched a future in which, unless she remained in the hospital under his care, her situation might be bleak indeed. "I could be stuck back into some prison with lousy food, heavy emotional pressures, and inadequate care, he said. And the same cycle could start all over again. Only how could I be sure I would be so lucky next time?"

Whatever his intentions, the surgeon had shaken up Patty badly. The way she interpreted it, the doctor was saying that he and his associates could cure her, but to what purpose? She would only be shipped back behind bars and neglected there. It sounded to her like a hopeless future, and I had to admit to myself that it didn't sound so good to me, either.

We didn't talk much; I figured this was one of those situations from which Patty would bounce back herself.

So far, she had always been able to reach back into that reserve core of strength that sustained her.

The next day, Easter Sunday, she was under stronger medication, and complained of feeling tired. Her parents came to visit, but didn't stay very long; they agreed to put off their holiday celebration together until the following day, when perhaps Patty would be feeling better.

Monday afternoon they were on hand again, laden with all sorts of goodies. The usual procedure when visitors arrived was for a nurse to knock on the door and announce them to me; I would check with Patty to see if she had medical business coming up, or was ready to receive socially.

I told her her parents were out in the corridor: "And they've got a stack of presents for you."

"I don't want to see them," said Patty.

"What?"

Very deliberately, she repeated: "I don't want to see them." And she clamped her jaws shut.

I went out and gave the word to the Hearsts.

"She doesn't want to—?" Randy Hearst echoed. He seemed hurt, baffled.

I felt badly for him. "I'm sorry, Mr. Hearst."

"What's wrong with her?"

"I don't know. I'll try to find out."

I went back to the sickroom, feeling very much the helpless dummy caught in the middle, and asked Patty why.

"I just don't." Again the grim turning-off.

Back to the hall I went, relaying the message: "She's not saying why. She just doesn't."

"Doesn't she love us?"

Gritting my teeth, feeling like some kind of human shuttle-car, I made one last try with Patty. Didn't she love her parents?

She did, she said, but she still didn't want to see them. I passed along that dubious reassurance, and sent word of the deadlock to Al Johnson in the waiting room upstairs.

Al came down and hustled in to Patty's room. He came out after a few minutes and motioned the Hearsts in: "Give her the presents; but don't stay more than ten minutes."

Patty's father and mother came in, almost timidly, with me behind them. They showed Patty the Easter eggs and baskets, the books and sweets and clothes they had brought. She accepted the gifts politely but without any real enthusiasm. Nobody mentioned the previous impasse. There was some random conversation for a few minutes, a dutiful kiss or two, and the Hearsts left.

As they stood around in the corridor—still hurt, still baffled—Al Johnson buzzed up, trying to make sure nobody went away carrying a grievance against Patty.

And that's where he and I parted company. In my book, there are times when being supersupportive is simply indulgent; when what the offender needs is not a sympathetic pat on the back but a good stiff kick in the tail.

Anyway, the fact is that at that moment I wasn't thinking of what would be good for Patty. I was mad; mad at her casual dismissal of a parental devotion that I would have given anything to possess. Here was I, practically banned, as I saw it, from the warm familial table; while Patty's parents came showering her with affection—and got a bellyful of nothing for their pains.

It was just too much. I pushed open her door and marched in.

"Everything I ever heard about you," I began, "all the things people were saying about your coldness and self-ishness, that I kept denying . . . well, I should have been listening, not denying.

"You don't give a damn about your parents, you don't care about all the people in the Service who are knocking themselves out for you. What you said last night about all of us being here on account of you is true. There must be ten guys on duty here who could be home with their families. Guys with small children.

"Here you are, a grownup. Easter probably doesn't mean a thing to you. But to people with little kids, it does. It's important. But do you give a damn about that? Not at all. If it isn't for Patty Hearst, it doesn't count.

"I really see you now the way you look to a lot of people: the spoiled little rich brat, the selfish little bitch. I didn't see those things before—I guess I didn't want to. I used to feel sorry for you, Patty, but not any more. In fact, I couldn't care less. From here on in, you're on your own. If you want something, I'll get it for you. But that's it. I don't want to talk to you. I'm sick of you. I feel like leaving you here by yourself, and taking all these guys with me so they can be home for Easter!"

I let her have it, Latin-style, all stops out; and Patty didn't open her mouth through the whole tirade. She just lay there watching me, as if half-hypnotized, with a kind of little-girl guilt on her face.

The next morning, she was full of apologies: "I'm sorry, Janey; I was wrong. I was getting uptight about my privacy, about never having a minute to myself—but that's no excuse for turning away my parents." She was

143

feeling like an animal on parade, she said: doctors poking at her, nurses sliding in and out, deputy marshals hovering around . . . she longed for an undisturbed sleep.

Even as she was making her explanation, a nurse's aide came bustling by: would Miss Hearst like a nice back rub? This same attendant had barged in, with her transparent excuses for getting a close-up of Patty, three times since breakfast. I lost my temper. "Don't you have any other patients in this hospital?" I exploded. "Get out—and stay out!"

With her family, the problem was more delicate. Patty wanted to see them, but they kept popping in one at a time, so that over the course of a day she felt she had to be "entertaining" constantly—even if she had just taken a sleeping pill. That seemed to me, now that I had let loose my own frustrations, a reasonable complaint. "Why can't they all come together?" Patty wondered.

I talked to Al Johnson about it, he mentioned it to the Hearsts, and an informal schedule was worked out that made everybody more comfortable.

My outburst seemed to clear the air between Patty and me and, rather than create a rift, to prepare the way for a deepening of our relationship. As her strength started coming back, her humor returned with it.

One night, while she was still hooked up to the respirator, a furious wind was blowing outside. I peeked out through the always-drawn curtains at the big trees swaying over the parking lot a hundred feet away: "Wouldn't it be funny, Patty—I mean exciting—if the electricity in the hospital were blown out?"

"Sure, Deputy. Real exciting." She glanced over

wryly at the machine pumping air into her lungs. "Especially for me."

She could find fun at her own expense, and even over the unfunny fact that she was still considered a likely target for terrorist vengeance. One afternoon I started out of the room in search of a matron who might relieve me for a while.

"You're leaving me alone," Patty pointed out. "What if something happened while you're away?"

"I don't know what I would do. Panic, probably."

Patty smiled. "Don't worry, Deputy. I could probably handle it—after all the training I've had with guns!"

Our weapons were kept outside the room: a potent arsenal, Al Johnson had assured Patty. When she expressed curiosity about them, Glen Robinson volunteered to bring in a sample. He returned with a toy machine gun he had bought for his little boy. Patty roared with the rest of us.

A new matron, the niece of one of the deputies, was coming on for that evening's shift. Glen suggested that we hide the plastic machine gun under Patty's cover. Patty would pretend to be asleep. Then, as the new girl settled in—

Patty finished it up for him: "I whip out the gun, point it at her, and yell 'SLA!'"

At the other extreme were her very firm and sober views on religion. Ever since her arrest, Patty had been receiving regular visits from the Rev. Edward Dumke, an old family friend. Although the Hearsts had been Catholic for generations, she preferred the Episcopal rites and counseling offered by Father Dumke, assistant to the dean of Trinity Cathedral in Sacramento.

She explained to me why: in Patty's view, the Epis-

145

copalians were more oriented to individual spiritual needs, took a greater interest in the personal problems of communicants; she described Father Dumke as "the greatest." And she found Episcopal theology more consistent, less willing to accommodate to shifts in popular taste.

Over the long hours we spent in the hospital room together, small oddities of Patty's also emerged, such as her love of animals. A pet gray cat had been scooped up by the FBI at the apartment she shared with Wendy Yoshimura, and taken "into custody"; she displayed no less than four pictures of him in her room.

I became more aware also of her sensitivity to beauty, both in art and nature. On our drives to and from Federal Court she had rhapsodized over snow scenes and the birds clustered in roadside ponds; now she reveled in the scents of the flowers filling the room, and showed me pictures of her favorite Oriental paintings and hangings.

That same sensitivity, I suppose, was behind her recurrent moods. She could jump from playful chattiness to sudden long silences—at which point it seemed best to leave her alone. We all need some time to ourselves; and people under constant guard, who aren't allowed even to go to the bathroom by themselves, need it more than most. I tried to warn incoming deputies not to take these withdrawals personally. Most of them were skeptical; they thought I was trying to preserve my special intimacy with Patty from potential "rivals."

Some of her preoccupation, I'm sure, was with her future in court. Her first trial was still part of a "dream from which I can't wake up"; the next one, scheduled for Los Angeles, would be "hardly worth going to." She faced a battery of complaints ranging from felony auto theft up through assault and armed robbery to the very serious charge of kidnapping. Patty felt that a negative verdict—with its possibility of fifteen years to life in jail—was preordained: "Everybody made up their minds about me two years ago."

And yet, in the middle of these broodings, she was capable of sudden concern for others: "Are you feeling all right, Janey? You don't look so good to me. I don't think you're getting enough sleep."

Patty had her self-centered moments. But one thing they did not include, in spite of magazine reports to the contrary, was illusions of Hollywood-flavored glory. I remember the time Al Johnson brought a picture to the hospital in which one of the deputies had been photographed with Patty; the deputy wanted her to sign it.

Patty pushed the picture away. "I'm not going to sign that thing! It's like a movie star—and I'm *not* a movie star." The ritual offended her sense of honesty. She also thought the whole business of collecting autographs was crazy: "When we were young, there were prominent people coming to the house all the time. I'm sure we could have gotten their autographs, but we wouldn't bother them. We thought of them as friends of the family."

Yet Patty herself was a collector of sorts. *Things* were surprisingly important to her. And they didn't have to be things of obvious value.

One of the Easter gifts from her father was a basket of flowers with a cute little duck sitting on it. I really liked that duck, and asked Patty if I could have it.

"Uh-uh," she said. "No duck."

"Oh, come on. I dig that duck."

"Too bad."

"When you're asleep, I'm going to take it." Which I did that night, leaving my card, imprinted "United States Deputy Marshal," in its place.

The next morning I was greeted with an impatient, "Okay, Deputy, where's my duck?"

I tried to argue and bargain, but she wasn't having any. "Give me it back. The minute I woke up I looked for it. I knew you would have taken it. And sure enough you did."

After I returned the duck, she had something else for her collection: my calling card. It had a permanent niche in her address book.

While she was in jail, an admiring stranger kept sending her flowers—one every day. When she was taken to the hospital, he finally sent his picture. He was much, much older than Patty, and not particularly attractive, but she hung onto that picture carefully. When it was momentarily mislaid as she was packing to leave, she was much concerned: "I don't know the man, but he took the time to send a flower every day." And the trouble to acknowledge her as a person.

Also on her "things" list was a hanging plant brought in by her father. She knew she couldn't take it with her to prison when she left the hospital, so she asked me to look after it for her.

"By the time you get out of jail," I teased, "you won't recognize it. It's going to be full-grown."

"That's okay. Just don't kill it!"

Her sister Anne is a jewelry buff. One day she showed off an assortment of rings to Patty, mentioning that one had been lost by a friend who borrowed it. The friend couldn't understand why Anne was so upset, arguing

148

that it was "only a ring"; surely Anne could afford another.

Patty's reaction was swift and emphatic: "That's what's wrong with people. They don't understand that just because we have money—that money doesn't buy everything. There are some things money can't replace." In that remark I thought I heard echoes of an inner loneliness, perhaps of a childhood insulated by circumstance from the usual early attachments.

Yet the yearning for tokens of personal appreciation—did even the Olmec monkey-face to some degree fall under this heading?—was always sharply discriminating. You couldn't court her favor with bribes. She was quick to detect the self-serving motives behind some of the gifts brought to her; where there was no genuine feeling, she responded with indifference or even contempt.

A case in point was the jar of green olives sent to her in jail the previous Christmas by the FBI, which knew of her partiality for the fruit through their researches into her background. Patty felt that for an adversary to send such a gift was a breach of taste, a tactless reminder of the fact that under normal circumstances she would be enjoying the olives at home with her family.

She was not very fond of the FBI. I don't think she ever forgave them for not passing along the warning when her name was found on a potential-kidnap list in January of 1974. "The funny thing about the FBI," she told me, "is that they can handle the Mafia, they can deal with all kinds of ordinary criminals, but in my situation they were afraid, because terrorist groups were a new thing for them. If they had known better how to cope, some very bad things wouldn't have happened."

She tried very deliberately to keep her G-man inter-rogators at arm's length. "Next time I talk to them," she declared, "I'm going to make them call me 'Miss Hearst.' They're so cocky, they think they know everything that's going on—but when I started to fill them in, they were absolutely sitting on the edge of their chairs. Not to mention shitting in their pants."

That was one of Patty's very few four-letter words. It was not true that, as claimed by the Harrises, her vocabulary was so raw it had to be toned down. In fact, it became increasingly evident to me during her hospital stay that very little of the popular impression of Patty *was* true. The supposedly profane, irreligious radical, the wild-eyed slogan-shouting gunslinger who hated her family and practically everybody else, was in reality a shrewdly humorous young woman: religiously devout, refreshingly honest—and in big trouble.

My earlier perception of a three-level personality— bumptious and defiant on the surface, tenacious at the core, and pathetically vulnerable in between—was rein-forced. Patty's problems were not with her head—that was screwed on tight—but with personal and emotional relationships. Never having been obliged to make her own way, to examine people as part of the process of survival, she had remained incredibly naive and open to outside suggestion, especially from those whom she looked up to as authorities.

It was that vein of pliability, as cultivated by Al Johnson, that pitched her into an ugly confrontation with the United States Marshals Service—and me.

Toward the end of April, Patty was walking around freely and was obviously much improved. Her hospital stay, in a private room under heavy guard, had been adding unexpected outlays to an already extremely expensive trial, so Judge Carter was anxious to establish whether she could finish her convalescence in a prison institution with adequate medical facilities. There was some thought of moving her on Saturday, April 24, but tests could not be completed on that day.

Judge Carter set 7:00 P.M. Sunday as the deadline for submission of a formal medical report on the feasibility of Patty's being released. At that hour, the Marshals Service in San Francisco was notified that Dr. Weissberg had signed such a release. Thereupon Phil Krell called Jim Ledgwood, Sr., the deputy in charge of our hospital detail, and told him to move Patty at 9:00 A.M. Monday to the Federal Youth Center at Pleasanton, southeast of San Francisco. Pleasanton had modern clinical equipment, a hospital ward staffed with doctors and nurses, and plenty of guard officers.

Monday morning was sheer chaos. To begin with, an FBI team was on hand to continue the interrogation of Patty they had recently resumed; apparently Al Johnson had encouraged them to believe her departure would be postponed.

Al himself was storming through the corridors, insisting that the marshals had no right to move Patty. Every few minutes he would stick his head in her room: "You stay right here; I'm going to check this out." He told everybody who would listen—including Patty—that she was in no condition to be taken from the hospital. Any shift would be at the peril of her life.

I, meanwhile, had very little idea of what was going on. As a matter of policy, deputy marshals are given only the minimum information necessary for them to carry out their duties. My instructions were to "go in and tell her to get dressed." I assumed that meant for transference to the Metropolitan Correction Center at San Diego; it had been my plan, after delivering her to prison, to visit my mother near Los Angeles. But nobody had told me the trip was going to be made this morning, so I hadn't packed a suitcase. I was annoyed. Didn't my personal life count for anything?

Patty, having gotten an earful from Al, was of course not receptive to my "get dressed" order. She wanted to know why. I was in no position to tell her. As I was trying to explain that, Al charged through the door, commanding me to leave his client alone.

I went out to report to Ledgwood. He sent me back in, raising his voice in no uncertain terms.

For the next fifteen minutes Al and Jim Ledgwood kept running in and out of Patty's room like a couple of characters in a Mel Brooks movie, while I tried to persuade Patty to get dressed. Finally—it was now nearly eleven o'clock, and she had first been alerted to the move at nine—Ledgwood told Patty that if she didn't put her clothes on, he would have to wrap her in a blanket and *take* her out.

Al spluttered· some more, then advised Patty she'd better get dressed, rather than be removed in a gown. He went out to the corridor so she could have some privacy.

But five minutes later, when she had gotten as far as her underwear, he was back again. Patty was furious: "Would you get the hell out of here?"

I was pretty angry myself, in the face of all the instructions and counterinstructions. "I'm so mad at the Marshals Service I don't want to be part of it," I told Patty. "Nobody lets me know what's going on. I feel like an outcast, that I belong with you. Hell, *I'm* the prisoner!"

"Both of you, shut up!" yelled Al. He was a real sweetheart at winning friends.

I answered with a blunt brief suggestion as to what he could do and the reminder that he had no authority over me. Then all three of us were screaming at each other at once. Al's voice was loudest—he didn't want to hear "another word out of *anybody*"—but with that he departed so that Patty could finish dressing. Except that I was stuck with the packing, stacks of odds and ends, which if Al Johnson had been more cooperative could all have been done the night before.

There were two funny touches at the end, which sort of summed things up. The hospital had been superattentive in providing services; it seemed that whenever in doubt, they sent an extra nurse. As we were leaving, a doctor came in with pencil and paper and asked Patty for her address.

"What the hell for?" I demanded.

"We want to know where to bill her."

Apparently they thought Randolph Hearst would be picking up the tab. The doctor was visibly let down when I told him to take up the bill with my supervisor.

And Patty's "jacket," the file of her hospital record, couldn't be found. Al Johnson had carted it off. The Marshals Service had to get it back from him.

The wrangle over moving Patty from the hospital had left everybody worn out, physically and emotionally; there was very little conversation on the drive to Pleasanton, twenty miles southeast of Oakland. I checked Patty in at the Federal Youth Center and took her to her room. "Well—hang in there, Patty." That had

153

become our code phrase by now for the sympathy and affection that were so hard to express.

"Yeah—I know."

"I'm going to miss you."

"Me too."

I hugged her once, and left.

When I got back to San Francisco, I discovered that Pleasanton was to be just an overnight stop for Patty. I would have to get up at four o'clock the next morning to escort her down to San Diego, where she would enter the Metropolitan Correction Center and begin her prison term by undergoing several months of psychiatric study.

We arrived at Pleasanton around dawn the following day: two male deputies who would ride up front in the car that carried Patty and me, two more manning a back-up vehicle. I found Patty in her room. She hadn't had breakfast and was clearly in foul humor. I learned later that Al Johnson had been there the night before and given her an earful about the deputies being high-handed and indifferent to her health; according to his indignant account, which he repeated afterward to reporters, his client had in effect been carried off by force.

He had left Patty with explicit orders: "I'm not supposed to talk to any U.S. marshals."

Well, that was her business. If she wanted to sulk her way through a long, hot southward trip, I wouldn't try to stop her. We would be threading our way along Interstate Highway 5, less heavily traveled than the popular coastal highway 101. I figured we'd be on the road at least ten hours, so after we left the prison I exercised my option and took off Patty's handcuffs. That way her hands wouldn't get sweaty, and she'd have less trouble

154

eating and smoking. I'd put the cuffs back on when we reached San Diego.

Faithful to Al's orders, Patty didn't let out a peep. For a good three hours she just sat there, holding herself aloof, while the rest of us sang, listened to the radio, and made jokes. Every now and then I'd get off one of my dumb cracks, and look over at Patty; I could see that she wanted to laugh, but she wouldn't let herself. She declined even to get out when we made a rest room stop.

What broke the ice was a news bulletin that came over the radio about Steven Soliah. Patty had been through a tangled relationship with Soliah, the rangy, sandy-haired son of a high school track coach in the Los Angeles area. Himself a star runner at Humboldt State College (shades of that other Steven, Weed!), Soliah had dropped out in his junior year and dropped into the Bay Area underground, working irregularly as a house painter. At the time Patty was picked up by the FBI, she and the twenty-six-year-old Soliah were living together in the apartment she shared also with Wendy Yoshimura. Within hours Soliah too was taken into custody.

The following spring Soliah was charged with participation in an April 1975 bank robbery outside Sacramento, in the course of which a woman bystander had been killed. He went on trial at the end of March, a week after Patty's case had ended.

The fatal robbery, at a branch of the Crocker National Bank in suburban Carmichael, was one of the operations Patty had been discussing with the FBI since her conviction, and even before it; I remembered staying with her once for after-court interrogation in the final days of the trial. I knew she had given the government considerable detail (the *Sacramento Bee* later said she had listed eight participants in the Carmichael affair including the Harrises and Soliah, and had attributed to herself an "indirect role" as driver of one of the "switch" cars used in the getaway).

Now, according to the information crackling from the car radio, Soliah had been found not guilty. Patty reacted with tremendous shock. Then a kaleidoscope of emotions played across her face: confusion, something like relief, and finally anger. She looked out the window and started crying softly. "I can't believe it." she gasped. "I told the FBI everything that happened. Didn't they accept my story?" She had rarely seemed so agitated.

I reached out and took her hand. I didn't say anything because there was no point in feeding the curiosity of the deputies up front. Patty continued to weep quietly, holding tight to my fingers. "I don't know why I'm crying," she murmured. "I should be mad. What's wrong with me? If he had been found guilty, would I be crying, or happy? How would I feel? I just don't know. . . ."

I don't think Patty's involvement with Steve Soliah has ever been clear even to Patty herself. It's easy enough to string together a series of disconnected episodes—her first teenage fling at sex, Steven Weed, the Willie Wolfe thing, Steve Soliah—and create a surface impression of casual promiscuity. I leave that to the forensic "experts" of criminal justice.

My own feeling is that Soliah filled an urgent if temporary need. At the time Patty met him she was totally alone, on the run, terrified equally of Bill Harris and the grimly pursuing FBI. Here was a man in her own age bracket—not of similar background, to be sure—but sincere and gentle with her. He too was a fugitive, so she

156

felt a measure of safety with him. In her mind, wouldn't that all add up to "love"?

Later she came to see the situation differently. I arrived at the hospital one afternoon directly after she had apparently been discussing Soliah with Father Dumke. "You know," she mused, "you think what you feel for somebody is 'love'; then you're away from that person awhile, and you see he's not all that great." Still, she conceded, maybe she did "have something once" with Soliah. I had heard her speak in a similar vein about Steven Weed—although never about Willie Wolfe.

Rolling along in the car, it seemed to me she had reason to be confused. A man who had shared her bed was going to be spared the trauma of imprisonment. Yet her sworn word had been cast aside lightly; what did that augur for her future prospects in court? And where was the justice in turning Steve Soliah loose, but condemning Patty Hearst to years behind bars?

It was a hopeless morass, a puzzle to which there were no good answers. Once again I had the sensation of watching a doomed bull in the *correo*; even when it came to her feelings, whichever way Patty turned she was trapped.

At least the Soliah announcement had the effect of canceling out Al Johnson's ban on conversation. However, we held off from serious discussion until we were in the Southland suburbs of Los Angeles. I had been warned by Glen Robinson against any demonstration of emotion before the other deputies, and I wanted to be sure we had some privacy before saying our goodbyes.

That opportunity finally came when we made our last rest room stop. It was in Van Nuys, less than a mile from

157

my mother's house. In the women's washroom, out of sight and earshot of the two men, I told Patty this was going to be our last chance for an intimate talk, and I had a couple of things I wanted to say to her:

"I've tried to avoid imposing myself on you—" I began, "telling you what to do, poking at you with questions. Whatever you've said to me is what you wanted to say.

"But you have to realize, Patty, that you're not a baby any more. You're twenty-two-years-old, a grown woman. You can't accept as gospel everything people tell you—which you have a habit of doing.

"Al Johnson told you to hate us—so you hated us. Just like that. No questioning, no sense of your own responsibility. The fact is, it wasn't the marshals who decided it was time to move you from the hospital; it was Judge Carter. He was concerned about the big bill that was being run up at the expense of the taxpayers, and he thought there ought to be some less costly alternative."

Patty was listening attentively, her eyes fixed on me. You could always enlist her interest with a logical presentation.

She had to understand, I went on, that people didn't generally operate out of careless whim or blind prejudice: "There are reasons for doing things. We didn't move you because we hate you, or wanted to put your life in danger. You should know better than that, Patty. We've spent so much time with you, giving the best we had to help you get through this ugly thing that happened. . . .

"It hasn't been easy for us. We tried to make you happy . . . no, not make you happy, but at least help you forget what was going on so you wouldn't go crazy . . . so

158

we *all* wouldn't go crazy with one another. We put in so much time and effort—and now you hate us?

"You've got to be grown up, Patty. You can't just believe everything that Al—or *anybody*—tells you. If you read something about me in the paper, for heaven's sake, don't just assume it's true; ask me first. And I'll do the same if I read something about you."

Patty dropped her head helplessly and began to cry again. I put my arms around her. "I'm going to miss you, Patty."

"I'll miss you, too."

"You've been exposed to so much in this case—tension, pressure, humiliation—it's a shame. Always rushing from place to place, chased by the papers and TV, your name bandied about . . . having to use a bedpan to get away from snoopers. . . . But that's the way people are. You'll have to keep on taking it.

"But the main thing is for you to be your own person; to realize that it's your life, not somebody else's; and that you have the right to do what *you* want to, for yourself."

The tears kept flowing. "I know, Janey. It's just—hard."

"I know it's hard. I had to learn it for myself, to grow up fast. Now it's happening to you. You're learning in a hard way—a *late* way—that you're not a baby any more. You can't go on believing everything people tell you."

Patty came out of that washroom rather shaken. The other deputies looked at her curiously, but didn't say anything.

I was going through some pretty disturbing feelings of my own. "Janey," I was reminding myself, "this isn't exactly a social occasion. Hell, girl, face up to it—she's a prisoner." A prisoner, but my friend.

159

11

The Metropolitan Correction Center, sleek and trim, rises twenty-four stories into the pale blue sky above San Diego, one of the few architectural landmarks of the city's downtown area. Less than three years old, it boasts indirect overhead lighting, tiled floors and a bright pink-and-yellow lobby. I don't mean to suggest that anyone would ever mistake the MCC for a Holiday Inn. Its monotonous exterior is broken only by two long lines of rectangular windows running from street to roof, about the width of archery slits in some ancient castle. No one has ever escaped.

Still, for its five-hundred-odd inmates it's an attractive facility, aimed at creating a "more humane atmosphere" than older institutions. The building is divided into eleven semiautonomous duplex units, usually grouped around a central recreational "common." Food is prepared in a downstairs restaurant and reheated by microwave oven on each floor; snacks are available from a commissary.

More than four-fifths of the inmates are male, most of them awaiting trial or sentencing; a relative handful are serving short terms. Because of San Diego's closeness to the Mexican border, in the spring of 1976 the prison population included many persons charged with illegal entry or narcotics-smuggling. And, as of April 27, Patty Hearst, remanded for psychiatric study before final sentencing.

Our unmarked green sedan pulled up at MCC in mid-afternoon, two-way radio bulletins heralding our arrival. Armed deputies were waiting at the top of the ramp leading down to the high-security basement entrance. At 3:35 P.M. the heavy steel gates clanged shut behind Patty Hearst, convicted felon, opening one more chapter in Patty's seemingly endless nightmare.

It was mid-afternoon, and the Center staff was changing shifts. Attendants and trusties were milling through the vast bare-walled basement; and, as everywhere, staring at my prisoner. I took Patty by the arm and steered her into the little entrance cage that screened off a private elevator.

At the hospital section on the third floor, we got out and worked our way through several winding corridors, past x-ray rooms and nursing stations. Patty, still convalescing, was unsteady on her feet. "Hang in there, Patty," I told her. "I know this place. There are a lot of nice people here. They'll be good to you."

The hospital room assigned to Patty was a 10 by 8 foot cell with a cot, washstand-shelf and toilet, and a glimpse to the south of the Coronado Bridge. I reached for my key and unlocked her handcuffs. Worn out by the long ride down, Patty collapsed on the bed. In her sleeveless beige sundress, Mexican-silver earrings and tan sandals, she looked like anybody's kid sister home from college for the weekend . . . except for the bloodless gray of her complexion and the drained, empty expression in her eyes. Away at last from the photographers, the gaping crowds, the cordons of armed guards, she let out a whimper of exhaustion.

"You'll be okay now," I told her. "A little sleep will make a lot of difference."

A doctor came in to give her a brief routine check. After he left I put my arms around her. "This is it, Patty. I have to go now."

She held on for a moment, hugging me very tight. "Thank you, Janey. Thank you for everything."

"Hang in there," I repeated for maybe the hundredth time.

She answered with a nod, and a wan smile touched her face. As I waved from the door, she lifted her downcast eyes. Her head came up, the frail shoulders snapped back proudly. Looking back, I can see her still: 110 pounds of weary courage.

I turned away and went downstairs. A deputy U.S. marshal doesn't cry before her male colleagues, especially over a prisoner. Even if the prisoner is her friend.

After dropping Patty off at the MCC, I had no direct contact with her for several weeks. However, Al Johnson kept me informed; he indicated she was getting along nicely.

On June 17, I took a prisoner down from San Francisco, and was told I could drop in on Patty. Her parents were visiting her on the hospital floor, and we all had quite an emotional reunion, with much embracing and—among the females at least—many tears.

Something had come up in the meantime that I wanted to discuss with Patty, but I didn't quite know how to handle: I had been approached to write this book. Under no circumstances was I going to tell her story

162

without her full permission; but, remembering her resentment of Steven Weed's account, I hesitated to ask for it. What if she reacted in anger to the very idea? I didn't want to risk losing her friendship.

As I was preparing to go, Lee Bailey turned up. He had always said he would be available if I ever needed advice. Well, I needed it. We were both flying back to Los Angeles that afternoon, and on the way I outlined my dilemma.

Lee didn't see any problem. "I'll talk to Patty about it," he said, "but personally I think it's a great idea. People don't really understand what she's been through, the way you and I do. And you're the one to tell them— being a woman, and from the same generation."

He must have followed through pretty quickly, because within the week he phoned me from New York to say that the project had Patty's full blessing. I could go ahead and plan my resignation from the Marshals Service—under federal regulations, a necessary move before writing. "Patty wishes you the best of luck," Bailey concluded. "She says she can't think of anything that would be better for you, in terms of your future."

I thought to myself, Isn't that just like Patty and me? Here am I, wondering what effect a book would have on her life—and all she's concerned about is what it will do for me. Patty made the point herself in a phone call on July 31, the day after I formally left the Service: "You're at a dead end, Janey. You're capable of much bigger responsibilities. And the Marshals Service doesn't make full use of your kindness, your ability to help others. I'm all for it."

After that, she started phoning regularly. Patty was running over with impressions and opinions on her prison experiences, and she couldn't wait to tell me about them.

To begin with, she thought her "ninety-day-study," administered by people working out of the warden's office, left a great deal to be desired. "Some of these people," she said, "have less education than I do. And I'd love to see *their* scores on an I.Q. test. Yet they're in a position to send prisoners away for life!"

She cited one high-ranking official who suggested that, in view of her interests, she might one day go back to school and study biology: "He didn't seem to realize I had already taken biology in college—and gotten straight A's in it!" Another examiner read aloud from a list of form questions: " 'Tell me, Miss Hearst,' " she mimicked, " 'what would you like to do when you get out of prison?' I should have answered, 'Run for Miss America!' Don't they have any conception of the problems I'm going to face, just coping?"

Patty's indignation wasn't confined to her own case. "It's the same all through the prison structure," she insisted. "Routine procedures, no real interest in individuals, nobody who levels with you. Guards, doctors—everybody talks about rehabilitation, where there is no such thing. How can you rehabilitate yourself without proper guidance?"

She agreed that we were overdue for an in-person chat. Patty said she would request official permission for me to visit. Two days later she called to report a flat turndown.

I decided to phone the warden myself—we had mutual friends—and he consented to see me in his office. "I assume," he began, "it's about Miss Hearst."

"That's right. I'd like to see her."

"What for? What's so important?"

"What's important is that we've spent a lot of time together, and we're close to each other. She needs somebody around who isn't always throwing questions at her, somebody she can relax with, friend to friend."

He toyed with some papers on his desk. "Well, what is her problem?" he asked finally. "Why did she get so worked up at me for not letting you see her? What's wrong with her?"

"Look," I told him, "I'm here for permission to see Patty—not to help you with a diagnosis. If you want me to help you, that's something else; let's get it on the record. But don't try to use me."

He drifted off into other subjects for a couple of minutes, then seemed to make up his mind. "Now that I've seen you," he said, "besides knowing all about you, I'd let you up in two minutes—if I could. But I can't."

On September 24, 1976, Patty was ordered back to San Francisco for sentencing. She had already been in jail for more than a year. The whole original cast reassembled in the huge ceremonial courtroom—lawyers, family, press, myself, even several jurors—with one major exception: Judge Oliver Carter had died of a heart attack on June 14. That was one more entry in Patty's ledger of bad breaks. At a private dinner meeting in the spring, Judge Carter had told a friend that ultimately he expected to sentence Patty to "something like six months."

He had been replaced by Judge William H. Orrick: almost literally a name pulled out of a hat. Orrick's initials had turned up in the envelope selected from a pile of twelve representing the federal judges of California's Northern District. Judge Orrick had been on the bench only two years; he might, I thought, feel obliged to prove he was tough. I was worried.

U.S. Attorney Jim Browning opened the proceedings with an ambiguous statement that touched all possible bases. Patty had been cooperative with the government since her conviction, he said, but she continued to "refuse to acknowledge her guilt, and perceives that all of her troubles are the result of the actions of others." It was necessary for deterrent purposes to establish that "rebellious young people who become revolutionaries, for whatever reason, and voluntarily commit criminal acts will be punished."

However, he suggested only that she should serve "some further time" (previously he had mentioned six years). And—most encouragingly—he recommended that the Court exercise its option of treating Patty under the so-called Youthful Offender Act, applicable to anyone up to twenty-six. This provided for a maximum term of six years, no more than four of them in jail, and eligibility for parole at any time.

Browning was followed for the defense by Al Johnson, who made a plea for leniency. Patty had been "brutalized, vilified, tortured, molested . . . punished, convicted and incarcerated," he said. "Your Honor, she has had enough."

Judge Orrick then pronounced sentence, a sentence that shocked the courtroom: seven years in prison, with no possibility of parole before sixteen months. "Violence," he told Patty without evident irony, "is unacceptable and cannot be tolerated." He rejected the government's recommendation of youthful-offender treatment because its purpose was to encourage rehabilitation, and he thought Patty had no need along those lines.

Afterward, I joined a half-dozen of the Hearst jurors who were lunching at Rocca's Restaurant. Three of them—Marilyn Wentz, Charlotte Conway and Dick Ellis (an alternate)—had been in the courtroom. Also at the table were Helen Westin, Beatrice Bowman, and Cloueta (Cleo) Royall.

The jurors were unanimous in their outrage at Orrick's sentence: "Why should one man—this judge who wasn't even there—be given a blank check to fill out as he pleases, depending on what side of the bed he got out of in the morning?" The only difference among them was as to whether Patty had already endured enough, or should have been given a token sentence of six months.

I shared their sense of frustration. Why should a jury, after undergoing months of sequestration and concentrated effort, not be consulted as to sentencing? Giving such wide latitude to the sentencing judge invites all sorts of nonjudicial considerations.

For instance, in Patty's case Jim Browning was reported to have backtracked from an earlier position of leniency after taking some soundings of public opinion. According to one magazine account, Browning told the Justice Department it might not be wise to buck the tide "if the people want to see Patty in jail."

And I ran into persistent stories, supposedly emanating from Judge Orrick's staff, claiming that as a new judge he had been heavily pressured from Washington not to go easy on Patty. The sources always retreated into a hasty "Don't quote me"; but there was no shortage of glib speculation. The presidential election was coming up in five weeks. The Ford Administration—so went the argument—courting the far-right Reaganites in their own party, would have had good reason to strike a four-square law-and-order pose, especially in California.

Now that her sentence was firm, Patty was transferred back to the ultramodern Federal Youth Center at Pleasanton. Located twenty miles southeast of Berkeley and about the same distance northeast of Stanford University at Palo Alto, Pleasanton could at first glance pass for another spacious California campus. Its clean white cedar-and-glass buildings, with low sweeping lines, are broken up by neat landscaping. The dorm-like rooms have full writing desks, and no outside locks; socializing is considered desirable. The 250 "residents," short-term prisoners between the ages of 18 and 26, are supervised by a staff of 140, including numerous noncustodial counselors.

There is an outdoor recreational area, a weekly movie, and an abundance of training in mechanical skills. Inmates can wear their own clothes and sit where they please in a cheerful, well-lighted dining room. They are even permitted "momentary" hand-holding with persons of the opposite sex, with whom there is free contact during work periods, therapy groups, and leisure. In short, the objective is to create a relaxed, permissive atmosphere that will promote the rehabilitation of young prisoners and ease their way back into the social mainstream: an ideal setting for 99 percent of the inmates, and by the same token a disastrous one for Patty.

Patty had been feeding the FBI information about some very dangerous people: information that could save human lives, head off property damage, and help defuse a reckless underground in a time of bombings, assassinations, hijackings and other extreme behavior.

Her revelations were certain to make a lot of people angry, people who through their involvement in prison activism had built up a network of allies in institutions all over the country. Furthermore, her enemies could easily infiltrate any prison they chose by arranging deliberately to get sent up for minor offenses.

It was a situation that called for maximum protection—and protection was the one thing Pleasanton didn't afford. It was set up along precisely opposite lines, to encourage casual mingling, informal exchange.

Patty put it to me very graphically, in a series of phone calls that began soon after she was admitted: "I'm a sitting duck here, Janey. Anybody can drive up to the parking lot and take a shot at me. At night, people are wandering around outside until nine o'clock, when it's pitch dark. I race back across the compound with my heart in my throat, straining to see if anybody is coming near. . . ." This, remember, is a thin 110-pound girl who in 1972 wrote to Steven Weed from Rome that she was "afraid to go out of the hotel alone" for fear of local wolves. According to Patty, Pleasanton was full of hidden menace, harboring "all kinds of little radicals, weirdoes," with ample facilities for making "any kinds of weapons they want."

Normally, she pointed out, a prisoner who turns State's evidence is put in protective custody. She wasn't, and her complaints were being ignored: "It's exactly what Bill and Emily Harris used to tell me—that if I was ever captured, the authorities wouldn't see my side, but only what they wanted to see."

I told her to hang in there, and not let the assembled bureaucracy get the best of her. She assured me she wouldn't: "I'm saving the best of me for my parents and

169

the friends who love me."

In her next call, she said she was spending a lot of time locked up in her room—not for lack of sociability, but out of fear. At mealtimes, she clung to the few friends she had made, but wasn't sure she could continue doing that. Other prisoners had been coming up to her dinner companions and sneering, "I see you like to eat with snitches"; she didn't want those who befriended her to be penalized for it.

Meanwhile, she was frantic with worry about who might be spying on her, unseen. Anybody could jog up behind her on the outdoor common and clobber her with a tennis racquet—or a homemade knife. It didn't even have to be a political enemy: prisoners have been known to strike out at other inmates who, they felt, had "got off easy." But we were both mainly concerned with the possibility that some SLA sympathizer would deliberately commit mail fraud, get a six-month sentence at Pleasanton, and take off after Patty.

It didn't make sense to me that the government would leave her exposed this way, unless—I wondered aloud—unless they were using her as a decoy, to see who came after her. Patty agreed that this might be a tactic for checking out her claims of being threatened. "I think," she added gloomily, "maybe the government wants me dead."

A few days later, to top off her fears, one of the professional counselors at Pleasanton bluntly advised Patty to stop cooperating with the FBI: "If you know what's good for you," he told her, "you won't testify at the trial of the Harrises—or anyone else." That was all Patty needed to convince her she was right. She wouldn't provide any testimony, she declared, in her present vulnerable position; if the government thought otherwise, they were "crazy."

Just as at MCC, Patty was eager for me to visit her at Pleasanton; in an early telephone conversation she said she was "counting on it." But although I told the warden's office I would come as a friend without pad or pencil, and they were welcome to monitor everything Patty and I said, again permission was denied.

More and more, I had the feeling that there was an unofficial closing of ranks against me, as if by exercising simple humanity on Patty's behalf I had somehow become a traitor to the government, a female Benedict Arnold. The attitude seemed to be not one of justice above all, but the "our side, their side" fixation of Richard Nixon or a college football game. And now in leaving the Marshals Service to write a book I had put myself completely beyond the pale.

Al Johnson wasn't much help. "I told them I had no objections to your seeing Patty," he insisted to me in one breath; and in the next, "Of course, I can't take any chances with complicating her situation." He explained to Patty that I was being barred because I had quit as a deputy; and to me, a few hours later, that the warden's office was "afraid of exploitation."

Patty was outraged at the ban against me. "I'd like to see the warden defend that ruling in open court. I'd like to hear his reasons!" It was typical of her that she would get more stirred up over what she saw as injustice to others than she would over her own case. When my boss, Chief Deputy Jack Brophy, was falsely accused of "leaking" the time of her departure from MCC to San Francisco for sentencing, Patty seethed in protest: "Don't they realize that information is available to many

171

people? Can't they find out who passed it on? I'm going to talk to Lee Bailey about it, see what I can do to help Brophy."

That impulse to lend a hand was very strong with Patty. It turned up on one of the psychological tests given her by Dr. Margaret Singer shortly after her capture. Asked to provide a spontaneous ending for the unfinished sentence, "My greatest ambition is . . . ," Patty without reflection wrote "to help people." I found her consistently interested in the problems of others, my own included. At Capwell's Department Store she had become involved in the rights of minority employees; at Pleasanton she was concerned with the rights of prison inmates. "There would be fewer tensions here," she told me on the phone, "if there were more rights and privileges; not only some extras added, but real implementation of the ones they're supposed to have."

Her compassion was real and enduring. At MCC, one of the corrections officers was married to a man who had an invalid child from a previous marriage. Patty broke off from her own troubles at Pleasanton to ask if I had seen Aida. How was her little boy? Were they still giving him only a year to live? Her voice could not have been softer if she had been talking of her own child.

And yet the pressures of her situation were creeping up on her. As she was walking across the grounds with Al Johnson, a male inmate coming from the opposite direction momentarily brushed against Patty. She glared. "Fuck off," she snapped. The man in turn flamed. For an instant Al thought he would attack both of them. But he walked on.

Next, news stories began popping up about Patty's "intransigence." She was supposedly refusing to go on

172

work details, "having tantrums," and generally kicking up a storm. Inmates obliged reporters with lurid accounts of Patty banging her forehead "viciously against the wall" and scratching her hands "ragged on the cement."

A couple of days later Patty called me, very calm, to explain: She had been advised that the only way to get shifted to the safety of isolation quarters was through having "incident reports" filed against her; so she had created a few "incidents," all of them highly colored in the retelling. "Wouldn't you say, Janey," she added drily, "I'm a little old for temper tantrums?"

At long last a compromise was reached: Patty would be officially taken into the Witness Security Program, under which the government would provide protection in exchange for information. To carry out the deal, she would be transferred back to the Metropolitan Correction Center in San Diego, where maximum security for her could be arranged.

It was a victory of sorts, but the prison bureaucracy seemed determined to make Patty pay for it. During the ten-hour ride southward on November 9, she was kept handcuffed all the way except for a very short lunch break at San Juan Capistrano; her wrists were sore for days. And when she arrived at MCC, the staff greeted her—in Patty's words—"like a bunch of ghouls."

Normally, prisoners under the Witness Security Program would be housed on the tightly shielded fifth floor. But there were no provisions for women there, so she was being sent back to the hospital section on the third floor. But this time, instead of the twenty-four-hour guard assigned previously, she would be totally alone. An officer would come by for an hourly peek.

From midnight to 8:00 A.M. she would be locked in her cell.

The warden conveyed this information, Patty said, with great relish, as if gloating over her plight. "You're going to be really alone, heh-heh-heh"—she imitated the snicker of a mustachioed melodrama villain—"do you think you can stand that?"

Patty felt he was trying to make her "beg" for a cell on the tenth floor, where women prisoners circulated freely with no officer in attendance.

"I'll stand it," she told him. "I feel like staying in one piece."

Patty was permitted no contact with the other hospital prisoners, and no recreation other than a weekly visit to the exercise area on the roof. A record was kept of every person to whom she telephoned—not regular practice—and her mail was tauntingly displayed, but not delivered; "you can't receive any," she was told. Visits from her parents were confined strictly to the official one-hour limit, despite the fact that extensions were granted to most prisoners whose visitors had traveled long distances.

As Patty saw it, she was being subjected to petty harassment because MCC officials were "scared of the spotlight," so worried about being charged with favoring the little rich girl that they leaned over backward to give her a hard time. She found the government attitude self-defensive and "sick." Her prosecutors, she told me again over the phone, were behaving exactly as the SLA had said they would; in fact, not very differently from the way the SLA *had*: this, in order to pander to public opinion.

But the public view was going to change, she predicted, as people began to understand "how much you can do to someone in a very short time through different kinds of torture." One day the full facts would emerge, and her tormentors would "all be caught with their pants down." When that happened, she hoped she would be able to accept their apologies with Christian charity, and not consign them all to the devil.

Basically, however, Patty was much more relaxed at MCC than she had been at Pleasanton; irritation was easier to live with than fear. She spent most of the day doing crewel embroidery figures, including a teddy bear and other animals, for small children in the family. And she read more than a dozen books, delivering capsule reviews to me over the telephone. In turn she was mildly interested in my enjoyment of *Citizen Hearst*, and agreed that she really should look at it one day.

As ever, she had a sharp eye for comedy. We talked once of the late Judge Carter's claim that he had known her as a child. That wasn't true, Patty said.

I reminded her that at any rate Carter was dead, while she was still living—"if you can call it that."

Patty laughed. "I'm a whole lot more alive than *he's* ever been!" If there was a tear under the laugh, we both ignored it.

Another time, I mentioned that I had spent the weekend letting off steam in Ensenada across the Lower California border. My dancing on the table in a tourist spot had brought some *Federales* running, and almost landed me in the brig.

"We could always get you out in a prisoner exchange," said Patty slyly. "Hearst for Jimenez. I'm sure the government would be glad to get rid of me."

No matter how she clowned about it, I was deeply

disturbed by her continued incarceration. I felt guilty, and said so, that I should be on the outside with new opportunities opening up, while she, who was responsible for my good fortune, remained behind bars.

Patty said I was wrong to feel that way. Then, after a long pause: "You know what? You think I've done a lot for you—but you don't realize what you're going to do for me, with your book. You're the only one who realizes what's gone on, on every side. Therefore, you can tell the truth. In other words, you're helping me, whether you know it or not."

A measure of relief was on the way for both of us. On November 19, Patty's attorneys struck pay dirt. After seventeen months as a captive and fugitive, followed by fourteen months more as a prisoner behind bars, she was released in Federal Court on $1,500,000 bail pending a ruling on her appeal. For the first time in two and a half years she would be restored to a familiar and loving environment. Patty would still be surrounded night and day by squads of armed guards, but at least she was going home.

12

Home for Patty was no longer suburban Hillsborough, but a sixth-floor penthouse to which her parents had moved atop the loftiest corner of Nob Hill. At 1001 California Street, it shared a sweeping view with the Mark Hopkins Hotel, the Fairmont, and the Pacific Union Club.

For thirty-six hours Patty luxuriated in the bosom of her family, drinking mai tai rum cocktails, making guacamole in the kitchen, and catching up on gossip with various cousins. On Sunday morning she phoned me in San Diego. High-pitched and bubbling over with animation, she sounded like a totally different person. She had "really been getting wasted," she giggled; it was such a delirious pleasure to sleep in her own bed, with nobody watching and no bed count to undergo at night.

How soon, she demanded, could I come up to see her? Never mind about a hotel; there was plenty of room in the apartment. Yes, she said; late tomorrow would be fine.

I hung up, aware of misgivings. Would Patty at home, in her own circle, be the same girl to whom I had become so attached? I had never quite forgotten Glen Robinson's warning about the contrast in our backgrounds. One reason I had turned down private guard duty with her (Mr. Hearst was paying $8 an hour) was out of the fear that I might find myself working for a stranger, a little rich girl I preferred not to know. There had been an incident or two at the hospital, after she was out of bed, when she absently relegated some chore to me, and I had to remind her that I wasn't her maid.

But the girl who came running to greet me the next day at Nob Hill was all affectionate generosity: impatient to share her private treasures, eager to draw me into the intimate family group. I knew nothing had changed between us when, as I was heading for the bathroom, Patty eyed me mischievously: "Shall I go with you, Deputy?"

The Hearsts were an amiable lot, with Patty's father setting a tone of mild bantering and his daughters joining in. Patty's sister Anne went out of her way to make me feel at home. Mrs. Hearst too was extremely cordial, in her reserved Southern belle fashion: "We'll never forget you, Janey, as long as we live; what a sweet and wonderful person you were to Patty when she couldn't have us. God sent you." Patty's mother brought tea, and served it herself. I noticed that, contrary to various reports of her aristocratic ways, she also did her own dishes.

Of course, there were small reminders that I was in a Nob Hill setting, and Patty was part of it. Displaying the bountiful baskets of flowers sent to her by her father's diplomat friends, Patty ticked off the names of the shops where they had been bought: only the best. Admiring my thick loop earrings, she turned to Mrs. Hearst: "Mom, do you think you can get something like that for

178

me at Tiffany's?" Mine were gold-filled, from Macy's.

But these were minor qualities in Patty, surface throwbacks to an indulged adolescence. It's true that this side is all she shows to many people; I suspect it's all she feels those people can understand.

We talked for hours, hardly able to realize that this meeting "on the outside," so wistfully anticipated during Patty's months in jail, was actually taking place. Around ten o'clock I wondered aloud if we might spread our wings and venture away from the apartment, perhaps have a drink at a nearby hotel?

Patty jumped at the idea: "Let me ask my dad."

Mr. Hearst and his wife had no objection. But Al Johnson, predictably, did. Even with a bodyguard detail patrolling us, he didn't think it would be safe. And he seemed to question the whole idea of Patty trying to resume a normal social life; was she ready, after everything that had happened to her?

Randolph Hearst finally talked him down. We would only be going across the street to the bar at the Mark Hopkins, and every security precaution would be taken. Al himself could go along, for extra insurance.

While Patty was changing clothes in another room, Mrs. Hearst came in. "I'm so glad you're doing this, Janey. It makes me happy to see Patty having fun again. . . ."

I thought I detected a note of anxiety. "Look, Mrs. Hearst, if you're worried—we can stay right here. I talked Patty into this, and I can just as well talk her out of it."

"No, no. I want her to get out and start doing things again. It's the best thing in the world for her; she needs it."

So we went out and had our fling at the Top O' the Mark. It was 2:00 A.M. before Patty and I got back, chattering away noisily, bursting into fits of merriment that we would have been hard put to explain. Patty's father, who'd been asleep for hours, stumbled out to see what was going on, rubbing his eyes. He took one look at the pair of us—we were doubled up with laughter—and started to laugh himself. If he had intended to complain about being awakened, he forgot about it. It was a most loving, warm reaction, and I loved him for it.

Patty's sisters, too, were very supportive, trying to get things flowing again on the old free-and-easy prekidnap basis. When Mrs. Hearst started to tell me how Patty was doing her full share around the house—making her own bed, cooking—Anne objected, "Oh, drop it, Ma; you make her sound like Goody Two Shoes."

The one thing that surprised me about all the sisters was their wardrobes. The open closets in the apartment were cluttered with dowdy hats, expensively trimmed but about as chic as an old pair of bedroom slippers. Like their parents, the Hearst girls were apparently unconscious of—or indifferent to—fashion.

On Wednesday, November 23—Thanksgiving eve—I was invited back to the Hearsts' for dinner, and stayed till midnight.

By this time Al Johnson had gone back East, which made things more relaxed for me. But before Al left, he and I had some heated words. I had felt for some time that Al was being overprotective of Patty, to a degree that was getting in the way of her recovery. In a discussion with me just before she was released on bail, Al had conceded that his solicitude might backfire: "Everybody has been running Patty's life from the time she was kidnapped, then thrown into prison . . . and I guess in a way I fall into that category, too. Maybe I *have* been taking too much of a hand. . . ."

Then he frowned and shook his head. "But I haven't meant to. It was an absolute necessity. I take nothing back."

And now that Patty was home, he still wasn't really budging. I called him on it: "It's scary for her, Al. Right now she has you, but someday she's not going to have you."

"I don't want to think about that day."

"You must realize, ultimately she'll have to live her own life without you."

"I dread when that day comes."

"What's going to happen when it finally does, Al— when she has to be on her own? She's going to be *so* scared. She's scared now; you're making her more scared. You have to let go, Al; you can't be there all the time. You have your own children; they need you. She has her parents. She's been away from them so long— separated by the press, a glass wall, a jail wall, bars, institutions—now that they're together, let them *be* together, find out about one another. How can they, with you always around? You have to let go of her."

Al listened, but he wouldn't agree. "I'm afraid for her. She was hurt once; I don't want to see her hurt again."

Having a hard time with Al Johnson was old stuff to me. What I didn't expect was the sudden flak from my friends. Patty's release on bail bothered a lot of people personally connected with prisoners who had not been so fortunate, although sent up on relatively minor charges. I was accused of being callous—a traitor to my

181

class—for lack of acquaintance with the sorrows of less affluent prisoners.

The accusers were wrong. I have a many-time "loser" in my own family, an uncle who's been in and out of prisons for most of my adult life. I've seen up close the hypocrisy and futility of our "justice" system; but that doesn't make me think Patty should have to pay for its shortcomings.

My distress over my uncle's story was undoubtedly a factor in my entering prison work. And Patty's similar response to the plight of her fellow-inmates was one of the things that drew us closer even after we were no longer in day-to-day contact.

An article in the *New York Times Magazine* in the spring of 1977 intimated that Patty looked upon the poor with patrician disdain; she was said to be "without strong inner principles or values," a nail-painting dabbler who "never expresses any interest" in social issues. In that case, why did she protest to me in so many telephone conversations the slipshod methods of prison "rehabilitation"? Why did she complain about the superficial quality of individual examinations, the indifference of officials to root causes, the willingness to pass judgment before all the facts were in?

Patty's innate humanity, coupled with her passion for thoroughness, made these matters of enormous interest to her. She sees prisons as boiling with tensions because they're filled with people who have no real understanding of how they got there. She wants to write about these things—but not yet. First there must be much more reading, study, reflection.

And more immediately, she would like to get her personal life back on some kind of even keel. Patty still looks forward to marriage and motherhood. When we approached our birthdays in the winter of 1977—Patty's twenty-third, my twenty-fourth—I remarked that it made me feel "more like a woman."

"Maybe I will, too," Patty threw in hopefully.

She said she'd met "quite a few people" over the Christmas holidays. I told her she was doing better than I was.

"Oh," said Patty, the disappointment evident in her voice. "it's just *meeting*."

Early in January, I brought a couple of fellows to the Nob Hill apartment, and we all went dancing. But the experiment didn't take too well. Patty was probably uptight to begin with, still a little rusty on the social side, and she had some problems adapting her rather formal dancing style to the raunchy beat of the hard-rock group.

Meanwhile, the "Patty Hearst case" was slowly taking on a different shape in the minds of many people—including the Hearst jury. The months following their March 1976 verdict brought severe stresses to at least four members of the panel: in the cases of Marilyn Wentz and Bruce Braunstein, the breakup of their marriages. By the time of their first anniversary reunion, the jurors were virtually unanimous (Marion Abe was absent) in agreeing that if a vote were taken today, they would find Patty not guilty.

Bruce Braunstein explained it this way: "On the strength of our own experiences over the past year, of now realizing the drastic effects of a change from one's normal environment, we could never convict Patty again." According to Bruce, the sequestering process

183

itself, by which the jury was cut off for six and a half weeks from all familiar associations, is now perceived by them as not unlike Patty's experience at the hands of the SLA. "We were put into an artificial setting, where the government was 'protecting' us twenty-four hours a day—monitoring every move, seeing where we went, what we ate. It's dehumanizing; you're moved around like a chess piece, you forget to have feelings."

Furthermore, argued Bruce, the sequestering had the effect of subtly lining up the jury on the side of the prosecution: "You're constantly in the company of deputy marshals and other government officers; you hear them talk about 'criminals,' people on the other side of the fence, and you unconsciously identify with them . . . until you're practically thinking of yourself as an arm of the court, and the defendant becomes for you a criminal!"

Other jurors confirmed that, with the passage of time, Patty's gun-wielding and even her witness-stand remoteness seemed more comprehensible; they were beginning to grasp that the mask she wore covered very deep, hidden wounds, still too raw for exposure. They were ready to concede that two months in a terrorists' closet, blindfolded, could have effects beyond their earlier imagining.

In the spring of 1977 came evidence that the jurors were not alone in their afterthoughts. Patty, although free on bail from her seven-year sentence in San Francisco pending a decision on her appeal, was still awaiting trial in Los Angeles for the fracas at Mel's Sporting Goods store. The Harrises had been convicted in the case the previous August on five counts of kidnapping with firearms, armed robbery, and felonious assault, and given sentences of eleven years to life.

On April 18 the District Attorney of Los Angeles County agreed to drop nine of the lesser charges against Patty in exchange for a no-contest plea on the serious counts of armed robbery and assault with a deadly weapon. This was a routine bargaining procedure available to any defendant; it left Patty facing a possible prison term of from 15½ years to life.

However, when she appeared for sentencing three weeks later in Superior Court, Judge E. Talbot Callister ruled that in his opinion Patty had never willingly joined the SLA. Since she had "no record of prior criminality," had undergone "fifty-seven days of horrible torture" as a kidnap victim, and was not "a present or future threat to society," he accepted the recommendation of the district attorney and put her on five years' probation. "I don't think there is a heart in America," he commented, "not full of compassion for the parents."

Perhaps. But there were quite a few not ready to bleed for Patty. Some hearts—and minds—had snapped shut with the first headlines, and have never been open since. I'm thinking of the people who to this day, in the face of captured SLA documents, the graphic accounts of Steven Weed and other witnesses, and the bullet-pocked doorway of Patty's Berkeley apartment will still tell you that she engineered the whole kidnapping—complete with her own brutal beating.

Many older but not necessarily wiser heads felt let down by Judge Callister, although he had the backing not only of the Los Angeles prosecutor but of Patty's probation officer. I suspect that a lot of parents, frustrated by failures with their own children, had fixed on Patty as a kind of substitute daughter, available for the punishment they could not impose at home. Her conviction and sentencing in San Francisco had given them rich satisfaction, as in effect a public pronouncement that beleaguered fathers and mothers had had enough, that there would be no more toleration of rebellious nonsense. This group didn't like to see the scapegoat get away.

So when editorials of protest against Judge Callister's decision appeared, there were readers quick to agree. Objections were raised to treating her differently from the Harrises, as if no distinction should be made between alleged kidnappers and kidnappee. These people did not know the facts and did not want to hear them. They had come for a lynching. They felt cheated and wanted their money back.

But most Americans, I think, are moving toward a different consensus.

The future, I am sure, will bring even clearer understanding of Patty's misfortune. In recent months, keeping an eye out myself for instances of forcible "mind control," I have run into a surprising amount of material on the crippling effects of systematic "persuasion." My desk is covered with clippings about the legal battle between the Unification Church of the Rev. Sun Myung Moon and parents of some of his young disciples; each side accuses the other of ruthless mental manipulation. A friend has told me of a new semidocumentary film from Canada, "Les Ordres," which dramatizes the psychic destruction of political prisoners through "humiliation, fear and loss of identity." And one of my former teachers, hearing of my searches, sent me a copy of Eugen Loebl's *My Mind on Trial*. Loebl, formerly a Czech Communist leader, describes the collapse of his defenses during the postwar Stalinist purge trials. After solitary confinement, sleeplessness, and relentless questioning, he writes, "I no longer felt that I was a human being."

On April 15, 1977, more than a year after the Hearst verdict, Dr. Louis West charged that Patty had not received a fair trial. The court-appointed UCLA psychiatrist told reporters on the staff of Jack Anderson that Judge Carter had allowed the government to introduce "bits of revolutionary doggerel" unconnected with the Hibernia Bank robbery, but had arbitrarily withheld from the jury the full text of the two-hundred-page West-Singer report portraying Patty as a "crushed, battered child."

During the trial, called to the stand by the defense, Dr. West had provided a lengthy narrative account of his observations while examining Patty. The details of this testimony, some of them to my mind fascinating, have been reported to the public only sketchily; so I am including in an appendix excerpts taken from the official transcript.

As Dr. West summed up his views for the Anderson people, Patty's "guilt" rested on three foundations: being a woman, alive, and a Hearst. She could not be forgiven, the doctor argued, for the "defilement" of having had sexual relations, however unwillingly, with her captors. She had failed to die, thereby becoming an inconvenience. And her cardinal crime, without which there would have been no kidnapping, no trial, no conviction, was the mistake of being born a Hearst. The sins of the grandfather were being visited upon the grandchild.

To which I would add the fact that she was young.

Puritan voices from the past were urging the jurors to "show that little upstart" she couldn't "get away with anything."

Other people acting under coercion have been forgiven. How else can we explain the paradox that American pilots who "confessed" under torture to germ warfare have never been prosecuted by the Air Force; that even in medieval times Jews who converted to Catholicism under the threats of the Spanish Inquisition were pardoned by their most pious co-religionists; but that Patty Hearst, alone, was subjected to merciless judgment?

I think the Hearst case has some unpleasant things to tell us about present-day America: our rejection of human values in favor of televised sensation; our galloping mistrust (the jurors didn't believe Patty partly because after Vietnam and Watergate and the nursing home scandals we have stopped believing very much in anything or each other); and above all, our unwillingness to look at the nasty cracks in our society: our seething prisons, drugs, unemployment, a crazy slate of priorities that makes millionaires of ball players but keeps cutting the budget for schools. We'd rather deal in platitudes than tackle our real problems. It's easier to comfort ourselves by "upholding the law" with a Patty Hearst while disregarding the message about the evil beneath the story, the festering despair that throws up, like mud from a geyser, a murderous "Cinque." But poverty and illness and a criminal response to hopelessness won't go away. America is a single community, whether we acknowledge it or not.

As for myself, the turbulent past year has brought

some good side-effects. Coming out of school, you tend to be on the cocky side, to think you don't need other people because you can handle everything by yourself. And you have a kind of narrow view of your family, without much awareness of how they got where they are.

I'm learning now that I need my family—especially my mother—and that the little gripes left over from childhood aren't as important as the love that flows, however quietly, between us.

Some of this realization came to me out of my experience with Patty and her parents. The upshot of it all has been that the long-time breach with my mother is closing: she recently made me a surprise gift of her cherished wedding-and-engagement-ring set.

My personal goals have not changed—only expanded —from what they were when I began work in the penal system two years ago. I'm still eager to help my people, but now within a broader framework of justice. For that, I must equip myself better, starting with a graduate degree in law administration.

Afterward, I see a long row of challenges ahead. I have questions about trial-by-jury, and about an adversary system that turns a courtroom into a dueling arena. I'd like to see better representation for minorities, including my own, in the places where decisions are made; stricter standards for prison officials; and an end to our "good guys–bad guys" approach to criminology.

I hope that one day Patty Hearst will join me in these efforts. Patty has been forced by the demands of her ordeal to develop a certain toughness which some people resent, but which had to be forged for her survival; the very diversity of our backgrounds might contribute to our effectiveness as a team.

Yet that day of joining will not, I know, come tomorrow. Patty must first heal her own wounds, reclaim the parts of herself driven away by terror. A recent news article noted that even now, when questioned by intimate friends about her SLA experience, "This look comes across her face. A screen comes down. Her face goes blank, totally flat." Patty herself may never be able to recapture the feelings that enveloped her on the day she entered the Hibernia Bank, so deep is the agony associated with it all, so crowded the overlay of subsequent events.

To arrive at some peace within herself, Patty is going to need all of her considerable courage, plus outside help and understanding. I hope people will finally let her be, set her loose from the Hearst insignia to become whatever she will. Instinct tells me she has a great deal to give; and, after her experience with the underside of American life, a strong reason to give it.

My most recent talk with Patty was full of the old rough-tender affection. I had been in San Francisco for a few hours on business, but did not get a chance to call her. The next morning my telephone rang: "Hey, Stinker, my spies tell me you were up here yesterday! Next time send me a telegram, so we can go out and tear up the town!"

It will be nice if Patty and I can move forward together. But even if our paths should diverge, I'll never be far in spirit from her corner. And I'll always remember her gallantry as my prisoner, her warming presence as my friend.

APPENDIX

The following was taken from the testimony of Dr. Louis J. West, court-appointed psychiatrist, under questioning by F. Lee Bailey, defense attorney. It is presented in narrative form with Bailey's questions omitted, and begins with Dr. West's description of Air Force training methods to prepare servicemen against enemy attempts to extract information forcibly.

"The men were lectured first about what to expect; the methods that the enemy used, the isolation, the threats, the abuse, but it was a training exercise and they understood that they weren't really going to be shot or tortured or that their friends and family back home murdered and so on. And yet, even so, in a—what was essentially a game there was a certain percentage who within a day or two or three of this kind of treatment would break down and begin to babble information that they should have kept secret and comply with the demands that these phony communists were making of them, even though it was obviously not a very good thing for their military records and so on. But in 72 hours there was always in every class a percentage of them who couldn't resist even that much of this particular type of stress. It caused a bit of a scandal at the time when word got around that men, American servicemen, were getting sick as part of a training exercise. And then we had to go back to consult with the Air Force to try to modify the program to make it less realistic in order to protect the trainees. . . .

"There were many who were weeping and unable to give a coherent account sometimes for weeks afterwards. Of course, this wasn't limited to the Air Force prisoners, and for that matter wasn't limited to the Korean War. The survivor syndrome of people from prison camps, POW camps and concentration camps is now very well documented and there is a high incidence of psychological damage done to people who are kept under captivity in this way. . . .

"I first saw Patricia Hearst on September 30, 1975. . . .

"I was one of a group of four professional people, two other psychiatrists and a clinical psychologist who were appointed by Judge Carter to a panel in order to carry out examinations of Patricia Hearst in order to determine what her mental state was and whether she was capable of standing trial and related questions. . . .

"I saw the defendant for approximately twenty-three hours, some of which—one session of which—was spent jointly with Doctor Margaret Thaler Singer, the clinical psychologist of our group with whom I worked very closely from the beginning and with whom I compared notes from her examination as well as my own. She spent seventeen hours. So, between us we spent about forty hours with Patricia Hearst in direct examination. . . .

" . . . in addition to our interviews with Patricia Hearst, I interviewed her parents jointly with Doctor Singer. I interviewed her sister, Anne, her sister, Vicki. I interviewed Mr. Steven Weed. I interviewed on several occasions Patricia Tobin and then I examined a great many materials including the bank robbery film, the SLA tapes, the jail tape of her conversation with Patricia Tobin and various documents that were captured which were shown to me by Mr. Browning and the people in the FBI.

"We saw Steven Weed's unpublished book manuscript and a variety of other stuff that turned up that proved to be rather less useful. I got information, records and statements by various observers, officers, caretakers who had looked after her and submitted their reports, the jailers and everything up until that time was made available to us according to the Judge's order. . . ."

Dr. West then was asked about what clinical observations he had made.

" ... to begin with, the patient seemed pale, very thin with a sort of strained facial expression, obviously frightened of the examination and on guard. However, there were no obvious signs of mental disturbance. She said hello, shook hands and was able to exchange a few pleasantries. She had no complaints. . . . But, as soon as I began to ask her for any information about her previous nineteen months' experience, it became extremely difficult. She would begin to cry. She wouldn't look at me sometimes through a whole interview. Her eyes were downcast. Her voice was almost inaudible and it was extremely difficult to get any information about what had happened to her. As I continued my efforts to discover what her experiences had been, what the history of her kidnapping was and compare notes with the other examiners, I found out that they were having the same problems or had had very similar difficulties. However, with reassurance and repeated interviews, gradually it was possible to get a little better information and then I began to see some findings that were very reminiscent of the survivor syndrome as we called it or some of the other victims that I had seen in the past.

"For example, each time I would come back to certain moments like the night of her kidnapping or what had happened to her when she was put into the closet, there would be the same kind of collapse. This was not only weeping and apparent inability to talk, but there would be a marked pallor of the face, especially around the nose and the mouth, very rapid pulse, sometimes going up as high as 140, which is twice the normal pulse, a cold clammy sweat would come over her and it was clear that this was someone who was terrorized or who was really experiencing some kind of a profound fear. Her ability to recall the sequences of events was extremely poor, and this difficulty did not begin sharply with the time that she was kidnapped, but it went back even to

193

the period before that. It was a patchy memory disturbance. There were things she could remember and other things that she couldn't, and there would be things that she could recall maybe after an hour or an hour and a half of careful questioning, and then you come back the next time and it was gone again; and I realized that what that meant was that she was sort of automatically pushing these things back out of her mind, which is characteristic of people who have been through certain kinds of ordeals.

"I reviewed the findings of the internist who had examined her and there were some biological abnormalities, not severe, but sufficient to cause some concern for which we never found any specific basis other than severe stress. The neurological examination showed there was no brain damage or disease, but the neurologist, in the course of his examination, observed the same kind of memory difficulties that we were, the psychiatrists were observing, and this was true also of the internist even though it involved things that had nothing to do with her legal situation, but with her health. In fact, she was quite concerned about her health, a very common finding in people who have survived prison camps. Every little bodily function becomes terribly important, sometimes for years afterwards. The ability of this patient to concentrate was markedly impaired. Simple tests that ought to have been easily carried out by a high school graduate or someone, anyone with her record in school, she couldn't accomplish. The IQ results that Dr. Singer obtained were not only surprisingly low, but—a full scale IQ of 109—but the pattern of the subtests within the IQ was distorted in a fashion that had been seen in other individuals, survivors of prison camps, and of other types of stress. We went back to find out what previous tests had been carried out on her through the schools and the national testing agencies which keep records, and found that her full scale IQ on two different occasions had been measured at 129, 130. This is significantly higher than the scores that we were getting and the difference couldn't be accounted for by chance or by different test forms. . . .

" . . . the total population has an IQ between 90 and 110, so 100 is the mean average, so her score was within the average range, but an IQ of 130 is within the upper 5 percent of the population and that's the kind of IQ you would expect to find in someone who, like Patricia Hearst, who had, for example, gotten straight A's in a full year's curriculum at Menlo College where she went instead of taking the senior year of high school."